C000183644

THE CROWN POST

By Paul H Rowney

Book 1 in The Crown Post series: 1485-1660.

One mediaeval house: five centuries of history, stories & adventures.

Imagine if a 500 year old house could reveal its secrets? What if one of the oldest houses in Bury St Edmunds finally told the stories of the people that lived in it? Their trials, tribulations, lives and deaths? Their struggles to survive the turbulent times Mediaeval life threw at them?

How were they affected by, or even involved in, some of the monumental historical events that Bury St Edmunds experienced? In *The Crown Post* author and former resident of the house, has woven a compelling and fascinating tale that combines factual occurrences with the fictional characters who might have lived in the (real) house.

Starting with its construction in 1485, through the Dissolution of Bury's magnificent Abbey, the bloody English Civil to the deadly Black Death and the infamous Witch trials, the house and its residents witnessed them all first hand.

This compelling and entertaining novel of historical fiction weaves the house, and its occupants with the rich history of Bury St Edmunds. The book brings alive what it was like to live through one of the most exciting times in English history.

Add in a touch of mediaeval witchcraft, which has terrible and tragic repercussions on any child born in the house and you have a captivating and absorbing read.

THE CROWN POST

The Crown Post is a work of fiction. Names, characters, businesses, events and all incidents are the products of the author's imagination.

Any resemblance to actual persons, living or dead, or actual events is purely coincidental.

Published by: PHR Media LLC, 197 Thompson Lane, Nashville,

TN 37211, USA.

Copyright © 2023 Paul Rowney, PHR Media LLC.

All rights reserved. No portion of this book may be reproduced in any form without permission from the publisher, except as permitted by U.S. copyright law.

For permissions contact: paul@phrmedia.com

For more information about my other books, please visit: www.paulhrowney.com

Cover design by Yeonwoo Baik.

Paperback ISBN: 979-8-9869861-7-3

THANKS & ACKNOWLEDGEMENTS

Thank you, as always, to my supportive family, who left me alone to pursue the idea of bringing my former home in Whiting street to life. A lot of things on the 'honey do' list remain, well, unfinished as a result.

Big thanks to my daughter Rachel who waded through an early draft and made numerous helpful suggestions on how to improve my initial efforts. To my long suffering editor Rebecca Taylor who spent countless hours correcting my errors. Any left in the book are of my subsequent making.

Also, my gratitude to the kind and helpful people at the Suffolk Archives in Bury St Edmunds.

A special shout out to David Addy whose mammoth (and never ending) history of Bury St Edmunds can be found in the *St Edmundsbury Chronicle*.** It is a work of such epic dedication I cannot begin to comprehend the amount of time he must have spent creating it. However, I am eternally grateful for his efforts, as they provided me with many ideas and much useful information. Thank you!

I should also mention two books which provided invaluable background to Bury's history: *The Sacred and Profound History of Bury St Edmunds* by Peter Bishop and *A History of Bury St Edmunds* by Frank Meeres.

Paul H Rowney

**http://www.stedmundsburychronicle.com/index.htm

CONTENTS

MAP OF BURY ST EDMUNDS IN THE 15 CENTURY

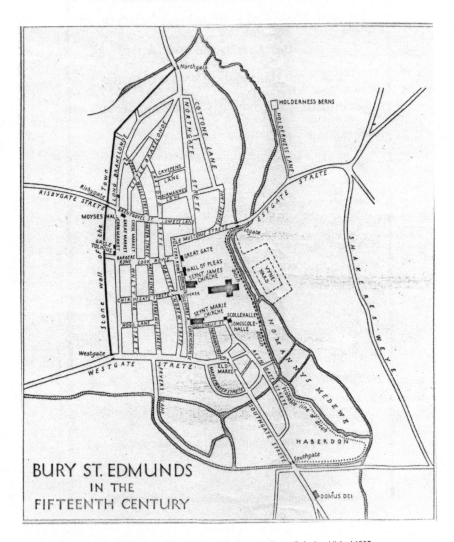

BURY ST. EDMUNDS
IN THE
FIFTEENTH CENTURY

Published in Mary Lobel's, "The Borough of Bury St Edmunds", Clarendon Press, Oxford, published 1935.
By permission of Oxford University Press.

Money in Medieval England was based upon 240 pence to the Pound.

Some coin names did change over the centuries, but broadly speaking were:

Farthing: ¼ of a penny

Half penny: ½ of a penny

Penny

Groat: 4 pence

Half groat: 2 pence

Shilling: 12 pence

Pound : 240 pence

Sovereign: One pound and one shilling (not in common circulation).

In addition, after 1549

Half crown: 30 pence

Crown: 60 pence

1500 currency (very) approximate value in 2023:

£1 in 1500 =£450 today or $600.

Introduction

The house depicted in this book is one I lived in during the early1970's as a teenager.

The idea of writing about its past occupants occurred much later in life and actually originated while renovating an old farmhouse in Lawshall (which also makes a cameo appearance in this book).

It set me thinking about who might have lived in my former 15th century home in Whiting street, Bury St Edmunds. (From a writer's perspective it offered more scope than my 16th century farmhouse in Lawshall!).

Not only is the Bury house over 500 hundred years old, but it is part of the first ever 'development' of houses based on a grid pattern-going back to 1080. An unbelievable heritage I was keen to explore.

Bury St Edmunds is a beautifully preserved medieval town It therefore offers a rich backdrop for the fictional characters in the book. Its long history and involvement in many major historical events meant its inhabitants-and those of the house in Whiting Street (or *Whyting street* as it was originally spelt)-,lived through exciting times.

This book tells their stories.

Prologue

~1485~

Witches aren't supposed to die happy, or old. But Spinster Wordsworth would do both. For nearly three decades she avoided the constant accusations of being a witch. The threats of a painful death if she were discovered, were always present. Whispered, gossiped, innuendos that made her life a constant misery. But the spinster survived. Now as old age made her body weak and filled with pain, after a lifetime of incriminations, abuse and hatred pointed at her, now it was time to plan a terrible revenge.

When it came to pass a monstrous and long lasting one it would be.

Months in the planning, as the final chapter of her life played out, vengeance would culminate in one deadly finale. The effects of which would be felt for generations into the future.

First in line would be the owners of the new house to be built when hers was demolished. Her home of forty years was to be carelessly torn down so some wealthy merchant could build a monument to greed in its place. It was the final straw. The ultimate indignity.

Her venom and retribution would then be aimed at children. For decades, these mean spirited youths with their pernicious and spiteful actions had made her life a constant misery. Spinster Wordsworth came to hate them all, believing they were the d evil incarnate, the sperm of Satan. For years, they had made her life wretched, leaving dead animals on her doorstep or piles of dung. Shouting insults, throwing stones at her door, killing her pets—their repertoire of petty and vile deeds seemed to know no end. Now she would exact her final, and lasting retribution.

She approached her death with a wry smile, Spinster Wordsworth had seen the Devil and he didn't scare her. In fact he was to become her ally. And as for God? Where had he been to offer her comfort and solace all these years? No, now was the time to let those who had tormented her suffer. Let them pray to their God for help, it would serve them no purpose, for he would be unable to save them.

The sweating sickness was draining her aging body of its life force. Before she dies, the Spinster hides her ancient *grimoire* of spells and incantations, handwritten in red ink from the blood of a cat. Appropriately as blood is associated with death, with pain. The cover is made with human skin. She carefully conceals it in an old well beneath the house. A place no one is likely to look for many years.

It is, in its own way, a creation of breathtaking malevolence or more precisely, a work of the darkest arts. The most telling of them all is a curse on the children to be born into this house of mammon, for the next 250 years. She has spent the waning days of her life working feverishly to collect the herbs, and numerous other ingredients, to create a potion, a spell so formidable its *puissant* would repel any attempts to reverse it.

Then, on a wooden tablet, she laboriously transcribes some ancient hexes, runes and symbols, finishing with a riddle, explaining to whoever may find her treasure trove of evil in the future why the house is full of such sorrow, suffering and pain:

In this house where a child is born,
A curse lingers, a witch's sworn.
Beware, young souls, its cruel root,
Their journey, a soundless one, a bitter mute.
Never to utter a spoken word,
Their voices will be forever unheard.
Others never to see or hear,
Living their lives in pain and fear.
For ten generations, this curse will last,
A payment for all the evil children past.

Finally, the long lasting, all powerful black magic would come from the days of maledictions she spent repeating around the house, the small carvings on beams inviting the Devil into the house, the hours of conjurations uttered, as her strength wanes such that she could barely leave her bed. These spells will seep the very essence, the spirit, of the house and *whatever might replace it.* As long as some part of it remains, the curse would survive.

She died, fittingly, on All Hallow's Eve, 1485, when the boundary between this world and the next becomes thin, enabling those who wish, to connect with the dead. When the living are at their most vulnerable, witchcraft and wizardry at its most potent. When the blackest of magic becomes real.

Chapter 1

~1486~

The Wars of the Roses lasted for over thirty years as two rival families, the Lancasters and Yorks fought over control of the English throne. Henry Tudor (later Henry VII) defeated and killed Richard III at Bosworth Field on August 22, 1485, bringing the civil war to a close. By his marriage to Edward IV's daughter, Elizabeth of York in 1486, Henry united the Yorkist and Lancastrian claims, thereby creating the new Tudor royal lineage, once and for all resolving their rival claims.

It is August in the year of our Lord 1486. The newly crowned King Henry VII is visiting the thriving Suffolk market town of Bury St Edmunds. Fresh from his recent victory at Bosworth, he is not, surprisingly, in an ebullient and generous mood. During his brief visit, he will be showering the Abbot of the Abbey with yet more power and prestige by conferring on him more immunities, land and honours.

Everyone is out celebrating the end of the civil war, which left the blood of ten thousand Englishmen spread across a dozen battlefields around England. Now peace and a new king reign.

People are joyous and relieved, no longer do they have to conceal their preference for the Yorks or Lancastrians, the country is united.

The new King was visiting Bury St Edmunds because it was one of the largest and wealthiest towns in the country. It was also an important economic and religious centre. The huge Abbey for centuries the focal point of Bury was the resting place of venerated St Edmund's remains.

In the ninth century, Edmund reigned King of East Anglia. In 869, the invading Danes killed him. During the tenth century, his remains were brought to the monastery for safekeeping. Once enshrined at Bury St Edmunds Abbey, the town became one of the most famous and wealthy pilgrimage destinations in England. As a result, the Abbey had immense power over every aspect of the town's activities and influence that extended across the whole of East Anglia. He needed its support and blessing.

The King paraded around the Great Market, across the Butter Market, then proceeded downhill towards the Abbey for a Thanksgiving mass. Practically the whole town of five thousand souls lined the streets to see their new King. Of course few will have seen him before, indeed most will never have seen any king or queen. Royal visits were a rarity to this part of the realm. All the more reason to celebrate. The joyous crowd looked up curiously at their new monarch, proud and aloof on his beautifully groomed white horse. He was tall, well built and strong. Many found his appearance attractive, with small blue eyes and a wide, disarming smile. Even at the age of thirty-one, his hair was thin and white, his complexion sallow. He waved to the cheering throng who responded enthusiastically to his attention, chanting 'God Save the King' at the top of their voices.

All along the route and around the square, the inns and food vendors were doing a brisk trade. Bury St Edmunds was a prosperous town, the people were out to have a good time, drink and eat, if they could afford it, many to excess. Everyone, at last, had a reason to rejoice after years of war.

However, not everyone was delighted to see the victorious King. Three miserable prisoners sat in the damp, vermin infested bowels of the Abbey. They were awaiting execution, due to take place after the King had left and returned to London. Accused of treason, the three were facing the most appalling form of death imaginable: being hung, drawn and quartered. A lengthy and painful process that saw the victim fastened to a wooden panel, and drawn by horse to the place of execution, where he would then hang (almost to the point of death), be taken down, emasculated, disembowelled, beheaded, and quartered (chopped into four pieces). Under the hands of a skilful executioner, this could last hours. One prisoner, Ian de Souza, prayed his brother, Sir Walter de Souza's pleas to the King for mercy, will be granted, sparing him the most horrendous of deaths. From their dungeon, the condemned prisoners heard the noise of the raucous crowd as the King approached the Abbey. Stuart bowed his head and prayed with a vehemence only a condemned man can.

Watching from the balcony of the Partridge Inn on Abbeygate Street, supping his third pint of mead, Sir Walter De Souza tried to hear, over the cheering crowds, his wife's worried question, 'Walter how hopeful are you your plea to save Ian's life will be endorsed by the Abbot? Before it is presented to the King?'

'I am reasonably confident, Katherine. I have donated hundreds of pounds to the Abbey, I certainly believe, indeed hope, my investment will be repaid. The Abbot knows if he ignores the generosity of local businessmen like myself, his future could be one of poverty.'

Katherine smiled at his optimism. 'I pray for his release, too. He is a boy who talks too much and unwisely, once the ale has taken over his tongue. He meant no harm to the King, I do hope the Abbot presses home your entreaties to the fullest.'

Sir Walter nodded in agreement, his brother was indeed a hot head, but not a threat to the King.

They both watched the King ride down the hill then pass under the stone arch supporting the huge Abbey gates, and disappear inside, followed by his retinue of guards and loyal aristocrats. The gates slammed shut, and with that, the crowd dispersed back to their homes, shops or for more merriment in the taverns and alehouses to be found on every street in the town.

Sir Walter turned to his wife, 'Katherine, shall we walk to view our new house, see if the builders are nearing completion? I am hoping so, they were close to finishing it a month ago.'

Katherine's eyes lit up with anticipation, 'Oh! Yes please, that's a wonderful idea! I am excited to see it. I love the countryside but it will be so much more convenient moving into the town.'

They walked arm in arm away from the noise and excited crowds, back through the market square, then turned into

Whyting Street, part of the grid of streets planned by Abbot Baldwin way back in 1080. They crossed Churchgate Street which runs down to the Norman Tower, the main gateway to the immense Abbey and its sprawling array of buildings, gardens and meadows, bordered by the River Lark. The streets were remarkably clean, courtesy of the King's visit. The Abbot decreed they should be sluiced down and cleared of all human and animal waste, rotting carcasses and rubbish. In addition, all wild dogs and other animals that normally roamed free must be killed or caged for the duration of the King's stay. It made for a pleasant walk, the normally pungent, unpleasant smells for a brief time absent.

As they approached their new home, they saw the central part from the original house was practically finished, the south and north wings were far from complete. The framework for the new roof was already in place with the huge Crown Post supporting it. Two builders scrambled across the beams fastening them together with thick wooden pegs. Inside, in between the substantial vertical oak beams was a framework of thin willow branches. Only one workman was mixing and applying the wattle and daub, a gooey mixture of clay, straw and horsehair that would fill these gaps and set hard in a day or two. Two others were dragging beams from the pile saved from the remains of Spinster Wordsworth's old house. It was common to reuse materials like expensive oak beams, and buy new ones once only as necessary. That, in total, was the activity at the house. The new owner was not impressed.

The last time Sir Walter visited there were over twenty workers. Where had they all gone?

Sir Walter's reaction, observing the slow progress, was one of intense displeasure. He had hoped it would be almost finished by now. He wanted answers. Sir Walter was a man used to getting his own way. He looked for the overseer, saw him on the roof and summoned him down.

Sir Walter dispensed with any welcoming formalities, immediately firing off a series of questions, 'Master Smythe, progress seems to be slow? Why is that? I was expecting the house to be finished by the autumn, that does not look likely now does it? Why has work almost stopped? Indeed, where are all the tradesmen?'

The overseer, a small, slight man in his forties with thinning grey hair and a long, gaunt face, wiped his sweaty face with a dirty kerchief, wondering how best to deliver the bad news.

'My Lord, there is a good reason for the delay. It is due to an…unfortunate accident to one of the workmen. One which has all of the others scared. Indeed, many have already left to work elsewhere.'

Sir Walter looked perplexed, his anger rising, 'Explain yourself man, you're talking in riddles. What has occurred to put you all so ill at ease?'

He motioned for them to move across the street, wanting to keep the conversation private.

'As you know my Lord, the previous house on this site was owned by an old lady. We found some strange symbols carved into some of the beams. No one could say what they meant, so we thought no more about it. Then two days ago we arrived at work, and found one of our workers dead inside the house. With a strange symbol carved into his cheek. It was one of the symbols we saw in the old house. There were other strange things done to the body sire, he had his ears cut off, eyes and tongue removed.'

'Oh the poor man, that is dreadful. You speak of a symbol...what kind of symbol?' Katherine asked, intrigued at this strange news.

The overseer's voice dropped to a whisper, 'It...it was of an upturned crucifix, my lady.'

Katherine turned to her husband, 'I don't understand what this all means, do you, husband?'

Hesitantly, he made the sign of the cross on himself, then explained in a whisper, 'These are the signs of the Devil, Katherine, of evil. It is possible the previous owner was a Satanist or a Witch.'

'Indeed, you could be right my lord, a passing priest who administered to the dead man confirmed it was a sign of the Devil," he paused, unsure of himself. 'What do we do now my Lord? Many of my men believe your new house is haunted or has an evil spell cast upon it, they are unwilling to work on it any further.'

Sir Walter finally lost his temper, 'This is ludicrous, the house isn't haunted, stop being so superstitious. Tell your men to get back to work at once!'

The builder shook his head, 'I cannot force them to come back here, sir. They are frightened. Maybe someone could come from the Abbey to dispel any evil spirits that may remain here?'

'God's blood! I will not have the work delayed any further. I will visit the Abbot and ask that a priest exorcize and then bless the house. Once done, I expect work to be completed by the year end, at latest. Otherwise I will ensure your reputation is so sullied you will find no more work in this town. Do I make myself clear?'

Katherine left the two men arguing on how best to persuade the absent builders to return. Always inquisitive, she walked over to the half finished house and the piles of materials stacked haphazardly along the street.

She reached down and ran her hands along one of the beams. It was a beautiful pale brown with a faint grain running lengthwise. One of the carpenters working nearby said, 'Beautiful beams of oak ma'am. Straight from the forest near Stowmarket. Please be careful of splinters ma'am we have yet to plane them to a smooth finish. They have only just arrived. They cost a pretty penny I can tell you.'

'I'm sure they did sir.' Katherine agreed then stopped at the end of one beam, noticing some numerals carved in the wood near the joint. "What are these numbers for?" She asked, noticing they were on all the beams.

The carpenter, delighted at the chance to explain his work, walked over. 'All the joints are numbered ma'am. We do that out in the forest as soon as the trees are cut down and we have cut the beams to length. Then we saw or riven, to the thickness we need, lay out the beams on the ground and arrange them in the order we'll use them to build the frame of the house. After that we start cutting the joints that will hold them all together.' He ran his fingers over the square end of one beam then pointed to the matching hole in another. 'See ma'am the beam with the mortice hole is numbered VIII, and so is the other beam with the tenon, or the tongue. That way we know which piece fits where. So we in a way build the house twice, once out in the woods, take it apart, then put it together again here.'

Katherine, who had never seen a house built, let alone walked around a builder's site, was in awe of the work involved, and the precision required. She saw a pile of smaller pieces of wood, some six inches in length. 'What are those for?' She enquired.

The carpenter picked one up and gave it to her. 'These are the pegs ma'am. See the holes on the joints? We hammer those in once they are together, the peg holds them in place, so your house won't fall apart, ma'am!'

'But the holes are round and the pegs square. How do they fit in?'

'There's the secret ma'am to a strong joint.' explained the carpenter feeling like a magician revealing his trick to the audience. "We hammer them in with a mallet with such force they become round, so tightly do they fit, they never come out!'

Impressed with the enthusiasm of the carpenter and his knowledge, Katherine continued her walk around the site. She looked back to see her husband still berating the hapless overseer. She decided to stay away a little longer. Stopping by a neat pile of the bigger beams, they were, she estimated, almost two feet square and ten feet long. Katherine asked.

'Do these large beams have a special purpose, they are bigger than any of the others?'

'Yes ma'am, they do. They are called sill plates. They are the foundation of your house ma'am, they sit atop a stone base to keep them from getting wet and rotting, then all the vertical wall beams slot into them. See, this one has the mortice holes already in it, and those over there are the smaller beams that will be the walls of your home.'
You are making me feel very confident our house will last five hundred years!' Katherine said, smiling at the carpenter, who was relishing the attention of this beautiful aristocratic woman.

'Oh indeed it should last longer than that ma'am. The house that once stood on this site we think was four hundred years old- and not so nearly well built.'

Katherine, side stepping all the builder's debris and tools, walked over to one of the finished walls and inspected an intricate lattice work of sticks woven between the beams. A man covered in mud was slapping handfuls of the sticky material onto the mesh of sticks. She stopped, standing far enough away to ensure she wasn't splashed.

'I have to ask sir, what is that awful looking stuff you are using?'

The man stopped for a moment and wiped his hands on his filthy coat and stood up. 'It's a mixture of clay, straw and um... horse shit, ma'am. We fix it on these willow sticks. It'll dry rock hard and keep the wind and rain out. Though you'll probably have to replace it every few years. Care to have a go ma'am!?'

Katherine grew up on a farm, and was not averse to getting her hands dirty, but dressed in her finery for the King's visit she decided it was not the day to get covered in mud, though it did look quite a satisfying activity.

She laughed, "Thank you for your kind offer, sir, but not today! I must be getting back to my husband. As she weaved her way through the piles of building materials she noticed a stack of dark coloured beams that looked older than all the others. She called across to the carpenter.
"What are they to be used for, they look different from the ones you have just shown me?"

Looking a little sheepish, in a quiet voice he explained. 'They are the ones we saved from the old house that was on this site. When we knocked it down we saved the best beams, and burnt the rest. Don't worry ma'am, these will be used in places that won't be seen, like the roof and floor supports. It saves time and money ma'am.'

'I would appreciate that sir, they are not very attractive.'

The carpenter agreed and doffing his cap made his way back to work. Katherine returned to her husband who, still looking upset but a little less angry, was warning the overseer he would be 'back next week to check on his progress'.

26

Without waiting for a reply, he turned to his wife, 'Katherine, you go back to the farm. I will visit the Abbot tomorrow, after the King has gone, and arrange for our house to be cleansed of any evil miasmas. I'll return in a day or two. Do not worry, all will be well. I will also ask about my brother.'

He walked with Katherine to the stables, made sure she was safely on her way then went into a nearby inn for some refreshment. He sat in a quiet corner and tried not to be concerned about the day's unsettling events. He had worked too long and hard, becoming wealthy and with influence in the town, for his handsome new home to be labelled a house of evil. He had to strangle this rumour before it could breathe into life causing damage to his reputation and business.

Despite most of the population becoming God fearing Catholics, people were still superstitious. Devilry, Satanism and Witchcraft were practised secretly by many, especially in the countryside. Sir Walter de Souza did not want his residence to be associated with such activities.

****

It took two frustrating days before Sir Walter was granted an audience with Abbot Thomas Rattlesden. As he hurried through the Norman Tower, he was confronted by a frenzy of activity as hundreds of workmen laboured on finishing the rebuilding of the Abbey, after an all consuming fire reduced it to rubble twenty years earlier. Weaving through piles of stones where an army of masons hammered them into perfect building blocks, he ducked under precariously insecure scaffolding and eventually was directed to the Abbot's chambers.

As he entered, the Abbot stood up to greet him, signalling for Sir Walter to sit down. He offered some wine. 'A little too early for me, Reverend Father. But thank you, and my gratitude for seeing me about this rather...delicate matter.'

'My pleasure Sir Walter. What can I do for you?'

He leant forward, unknowingly talking in little more than a whisper. He explained about the death at this house, the sign on the corpse's face, its mutilation. And the symbols found as they demolished the old lady's house to make way for his new home. He tried to sound concerned, but not panicked, about the whole matter. He ended his explanation asking the Abbot, 'Should I be worried Reverend Father, or is it something I should just ignore. Merely suspicious tittle tattle?'

The Abbot relaxed in his magnificent carved oak chair, which dated back to the early days of the Abbey in 1065, when it was made for Abbot Baldwin. To sit in it, still gave him a feeling of power, the majesty of his office. It was one of the few things that had survived the riots in 1327 which saw the original Abbey destroyed. At that time, the Abbey owned all of West Suffolk, it even ran the Royal Mint! The riot curbed some of the Abbey's excessive authority, but over the decades it had cunningly been reinstated. However, an accidental fire in 1465 had reduced the Abbey to ashes and curtailed its prosperity again. Now with the magnificent new building arising for a third time, Abbot Rattlesden was feeling at ease with the world. He supped his wine and pondered for a minute on Sir Walter's travails. He immediately realised he could obtain a handsome fee for exorcizing this rich man's house. Of more concern, was the obvious signs that some kind of Devil worship was active within the town.

'Sir Walter, of course I would be delighted to come and bless your new house and perform an exorcism. However, these are time consuming, therefore expensive, but I am sure a man of your wealth will be able to make a substantial donation...to the Abbey's rebuilding costs?'

Inwardly grimacing at the Abbot's blatant greed, he offered the sum of £10—what one of his workmen earn in a year, he thought bitterly. 'That is most, most generous of you Sir Walter, I will see to it immediately. Of more concern to me is the reappearance of what appears to be some kind of Satanic adherents in our parish. Do you, by chance, know the name of the dead man?'

'Yes, I believe he was called Henry Baldwin of Lawshall.'

'Thank you, I will make some enquiries among his family. In the meantime I would be grateful if you could keep this matter to yourself, until I know more?'

Sir Walter happily agreed to keep this whole matter confidential. He stood to leave, then, holding his breath, asked, 'Abbot, did, perchance, the King accept my plea for mercy on behalf of my wayward brother?'

'Ah yes, well there you are in luck Sir Walter. The king was in a munificent mood after his victory at Bosworth. He accepted your brother's digressions were the result of youthful exuberance and too much ale, that no harm was intended. In the spirit of reconciliation, he asked me to convey his wish that your brother be freed.'

Sir Walter breathed a huge sigh of relief. His brother was a loud mouthed liability, drinking too much and always upsetting someone. But he was kith and kin, and his only sibling. To have his life spared was a blessing.

'That is wonderful news and I am grateful for you interceding on my behalf. When will he be released?'

'You may collect him now if you wish?'

With a sly smile, Sir Walter replied, 'Actually, Reverend Father, let us teach him a small lesson. Could he remain as your guest for, say, another two days? An uncomfortable stay with the threat of execution hanging over his head might set him straight?'

'My pleasure, Sir Walter, sometimes these youngsters have to learn the hard way.'

A few days later, the Abbot himself performed a lengthy blessing on Sir Walter's house. Everyone who saw or heard about it, was impressed that the most senior figure from the Abbey had undertaken this assignment. Sir Walter must be a man of importance! A rumour he was happy to see spread around the town. Prestige was an invisible currency, but often worth more than any amount of pounds, shillings and pence. He was relieved. From a potentially awkward situation, something positive had arisen.

Within four months, the house was finished. A magnificent three story building, with expensive glass windows at the front, and beautiful wood floors throughout—both only to be found in the most wealthy person's abode. The exterior was whitewashed between the thick oak beams. It was the largest house on Whyting Street. The double frontage and tall pitched roofs showcased the very latest, and most expensive architectural styles. The southern wing, or gable, was for household activities —a huge inglenook fireplace with a stone mantle stood ready for use in the front room. The rear two rooms were for storage and food preparation. Upstairs, the servant's capacious quarters. A central hallway, or great hall, connected it to the north gable accessing the family's expansive living accommodation.

It was a grand house that held yet another secret besides the runes and *grimoire*: buried in one of the walls was a dead cat— put there by a superstitious worker as protection against evil spirits. It was a long held belief this Pagan act would ward off the Devil. However, despite the best of intentions, it would not prove to be effective. What Sir Walter didn't know is that in an effort to save time and money the overseer reused many of the large oak beams from the previous building, including the ones with the strange symbols carved upon them.

Meanwhile, Abbot Rattlesden made some discreet enquiries about the dead man, and the previous owner of Sir Walter's house. What he discovered both intrigued and worried him. He had heard whispers that the old lady named Emily Wordsworth, who owned the (now demolished) property in Whyting Street had long been suspected of being a witch, though nothing had been proven. While it didn't need much to make an accusation stick, as half sister to Thomas Spring III a hugely wealthy and powerful businessman living a few miles away in Long Melford, no one pursued the matter. It would have been foolhardy to rely on 'proof' such as her age, living alone and keeping cats for company, as reasons to imprison or even burn her. So she had been left untroubled by the authorities.

What intrigued the Abbot was the body found at the building site. Peasant Henry Baldwin, or at least his family, the local priest had informed him, were irregular church goers and generally of poor character. The priest described them as, 'UnGodly, unclean and unlikable.' Only Henry Baldwin's ability as a much in demand skilled carpenter kept his limited reputation intact. Gossip claimed strange activities occurred at their farm, but no one had taken too much notice. People kept themselves to themselves in the country. So why was he mutilated, murdered, with a Satanic sign carved on his face?

Was he a devil worshipper, killed in some kind of vigilante act, the sign left to indicate the killer knew of his nefarious activities? Or some Satanic killer with a grudge, trying to besmirch Baldwin's reputation or, more likely, Sir Walter's, by making it appear the Devil was to take up residence in the new house? But why? The Abbot asked the local Priest for regular updates on the family. Something was amiss, he just couldn't deduce what it was.

Chapter 2

~1486~

Henry Baldwin was a victim of the dark rivalry between members of two Covens. The cause? A dispute over land. For years, two families, the Baldwins and the Coopers argued and fought over a ten acre parcel of woodland— a valuable commodity in those days. Both claimed ownership based on a distant relative from whom they alleged a kinship. Over the years it spread from just the families involved, to their local Covens and Baldwin was a member of the Coven in Lawshall, a village south of Bury.

When a member of the opposing Cooper family (part of the Hawstead Coven) died under suspicious circumstances, his dead body carved with a satanic symbol on his cheek, his Coven, demanded revenge against the Baldwins. They suspected them of using witchcraft to kill their relative. Spinster Wordsworth, head witch of the Coven in Lawshall, became the target of their vendetta.

It was decided to kill Henry Baldwin while working on the new house where once stood Spinster Wordsworth's home. The head witch of the Hawstead Coven, Janet Farmer, also known as the 'Altar of the Circle' thought it appropriate, even ironic, to arrange the murder at her enemy's old house. It might deflect any connection with Hawstead and her Coven. She instructed two of her most loyal acolytes to kill him on his way home and dump the body at the house, leaving a clear mark that the 'devil had been involved.' Janet knew of Spinster Wordsworth's reputation in the town as a witch. She hoped by desecrating Baldwin's body in such a way, blame might be laid upon her. The fact she was dead mattered not. In an era where Witchcraft, Satanic rituals and the firm belief that evil forces could be used to great effect against an enemy, the manner of Baldwin's death would be believed by many as the work of the Devil. Creating suspicions, it was some kind of evil retribution for the demolition of her house.

Henry Baldwin's dead body, complete with Satanic markings also sent a deadly signal to the Lawshall Coven that the witches of Hawstead were not to be underestimated. While his death might not resolve the problem of the land's ownership, it made it clear that they would use all the powers at their disposal to win the dispute. And with the death of the Lawshall Coven's Altar of the Circle, Spinster Wordsworth, they now believed they had the upper hand in the fight.

Caught in the middle was Sir Walter, and his new house, unwitting participants in a battle between two forces of evil. One which they now saw on their own doorstep—and others hidden within the very fabric of the house arising from the remains of Spinster Wordsmith's old home.

Chapter 3

~1486~

Katherine, Sir Walter and his brother, Ian, celebrated Christmas 1486 in style with plenty to eat and drink. Friends came round to admire their handsome and spacious new house. Sir Walter's reputation was intact, his business was thriving. As tradition dictated, they placed a large log in the huge inglenook fireplace on Christmas Eve, decorating it with ribbons. After lighting, they kept it burning throughout the twelve days of Christmas. It was considered lucky to keep some of the charred remains to kindle the log the following year.

They hoped this new home, blessed by the Abbot, would be similarly blessed with children. It was not to be. By Spring 1487, the first epidemic of a mysterious illness known as Sweating Sickness invaded the town. Sir Walter succumbed first within hours of being infected. Katherine a few weeks later, a two month old baby in her womb, one that should it have been born would have had the most terrible afflictions.

The disease would reappear intermittently over the next three hundred years. No one knew exactly what caused it, and there was no treatment. The house now belonged to the dissolute brother, who after losing too many wagers at cards and dice in the local taverns sold it and moved back to the family farm in Woolpit. He complained bitterly that the house was cursed with bad luck.

Chapter 4

~1500~

The House passed through several owners after Ian de Souza sold it to pay off his gambling debts. For some, it proved too big and costly to maintain. Only fifteen years after it was built, much repair work needed to be done particularly to the roof which, claimed one builder, was the result of shoddy, hurried work when the house was built. A new Crown Post was installed to support the roof, and several mullion windows were replaced. It was an expensive house to own. A money lender, Justice of the Peace and a lawyer all came and went when the costs of keeping the house became too great a burden.

Finally, the hugely wealthy Duke of Northumberland bought it as his 'pied a terre', a place for secret liaisons with his latest mistress, a young girl called Phillipa Haviland. Previously a housemaid at his ancestral home, Barton Hall, he installed her in the house to be at his beck and call. Not surprisingly, Phillipa found the new house much to her taste. An improvement in her living standards beyond her wildest dreams. In practice, it was used more by his youngest son Sir William, for parties, gambling, drinking and entertaining his numerous bawdy, rich friends.

The Duke was a regular visitor when his wife was indisposed, a more frequent occurrence as she became ill and disabled with a mystery ague. In contrast to his sixty year old wife, Phillipa's taut, willing young body was a tonic for the septuagenarian aristocrat, who revelled in her uninhibited, energetic, sexual abilities. He found her inventive sexual performances tiring, but immensely satisfying. In addition, Phillipa's lively, intelligent conversation easily bridged the gap between a lowly servant girl and a crusty old aristocrat.

However, after some twelve months, the elderly Duke grew tired of her. His libidinous needs declined with age and recurring bouts of gout, made his performance in bed painful and at times embarrassing. Eventually he stopped visiting her at all. For weeks she remained at the house awaiting her fate.

Keen to maintain her comforts, before the bed had cooled from the Duke's last visit, the canny girl detected another opportunity. Used to the attentions of wealthy, powerful men— and the expensive gifts they bestowed even on humble servants like herself, she wanted to keep it that way. And she had her next benefactor in mind. Phillipa's target: The Duke's son, young Sir William.

She homed in on the unsuspecting young man with arrow-like precision. At nineteen years old, he was naive when it came to judging—or understanding—a woman's seductive wiles. At first, she flirted and played hard to get. Gradually reeling him in, like a skilled fisherman with a large catch on the hook. She captured his attention and desires with practised ease. Once he fell under her spell, he begged her to stay at the house and became his full time live-in lover.

She coyly agreed. A girl like Phillipa could only play hard to get for so long, make the chase too difficult and the hunter may go after easier prey. It was a bold, risky strategy. She knew only too well that if he tired of her, she would be out of the house and without doubt, unwelcome back to Barton Hall and without gainful employment. A life on the streets, or in the workhouse, was not a future Phillipa intended for herself.

He was, after just a few weeks, besotted with her. The gullible young aristocrat fell for her gamine good looks and adventurous escapades in bed. Fresh faced with fair skin, flowing blonde hair, he couldn't have cared less about her poor background and limited education. She had a delightfully open minded attitude to sex. Compared to the whores in the taverns he frequented she was willing, responsive, and a great teacher. Keeping him amused not just in the bedchamber but in light-hearted conversation as well.

She had to admit at times his demands verged on the insatiable. Though the practice did seem to be gradually improving his technique, thankfully, she thought as for the second time that evening, as he gently eased open her legs. Anxious to please him, she started to gently move her hips in perfect time with his. Allowing him to do as he wished, her body was his to use, it was the least she could do, and a sure way to keep him coming back for more. Just at times it was, well something of a chore, but one where the inconvenience was outweighed by the benefits. Of course, while in no way in love with him, he was, nevertheless, a handsome, virile young man. The sex more pleasurable (though a little quicker) than his seventy-five year old father.

39

As she brought them both towards a crescendo of pleasure, she thought herself fortunate to have such a willing and controllable man between her legs, providing her endless sexual gratification, and more prosaically, a comfortable place in which to live. Oh, to have such power over men!

Bringing herself back to the present, Phillipa whispered urgently in his ear, 'Yes, yes, William, now, now let us finish together.' She bucked her hips against his faster and faster. Clasping her legs around his waist, William arched his back and cried out, seemingly in pain, as he finished with one final thrust, collapsing on top of her, sweating and breathless.

As he lay motionless in a post coital trance, she mechanically stroked the back of his head, as one would a pet cat. He casually played with her breast and nipple, like a boy with a new toy. After a few moments he mumbled, 'My darling Phillipa, your body gives me so much satisfaction. Allow me just a few minutes and let us start again! I want you so badly!'

Reverting to a more formal mode of conversation, she gently pushed him off, 'My Lord, likewise I find your lovemaking skills pleasure me like no man before, but I need to take care of certain matters to avoid me becoming with child.' It was a well practised excuse, though a genuine one. She went to the adjoining room where a basin of liquid was ready for her use.. She squatted down and douched herself with water and vinegar, it was supposed to prevent pregnancy, so far it seemed to work. Having a child would ruin all her plans, and she was a long way from reaching the stage where she felt confident that she was ready to live outside the comfort of this grand house.

A few minutes later she came back to her room to find him dressing, 'You are leaving so soon, My Lord? I was hoping we might share some supper together?' In truth, she wasn't concerned if he stayed, or not, Phillipa enjoyed the quiet solitude of the large house, allowing her to occasionally entertain friends when he wasn't around. However, she knew he liked to be invited to linger with her, rarely keen to return to the cavernous, rigid, formality of Barton Hall.

'Reluctantly I must leave my darling, the Duke is entertaining tonight and my presence is requested. It will be a stuffy, boring affair I'm sure. Full of old farts and ugly women, 'tis not my idea of an enjoyable evening.' He walked up to Phillipa, held her tightly and kissed her lips, 'I only want to spend time with you. You are like laudanum to me. I am addicted, wanting more and more of you. Each time we make love, my body craves to repeat it.' Adding, somewhat melodramatically, 'I cannot get enough of you! Fear not my love I will be back tomorrow!'

Following him down through the great hall, she casually asked, 'What shall I do with the food I purchased from the market?'

The spoiled young man was dismissive, 'Give it to the poor!' Then realising what she really meant, dug into his pocket and left a pound coin on the table, 'Will that be sufficient?'

With a smile, or was it a slight smirk? She replied, 'That will be more than enough My Lord, I shall see to it that the food finds some hungry mouths to feed.' Phillipa knew Sir William wasn't being mean, just thoughtless. In the rarefied atmosphere of Barton Hall, aristocrats like him probably never paid for a meal, or food in their life. It just appeared at the dining table as if by magic. Other, unseen worker bees delivered it, cooked and served it, all without an aristocratic hand involved.

Along with the other gifts he bought her, this money was squirrelled away for the inevitable day when she would be discarded like an old coat. Pleasingly, her nest egg was approaching the level where it wouldn't matter.

That day came sooner than either of them could have possibly foreseen.

A week later, Sir William stumbled into the house, not just worse the wear for drink, but showing the obvious signs of being in a fight. He collapsed into the chair, exhausted, bruised and with several cuts around his face. His normally bright humour was absent.

Phillipa came back from the kitchen with a bowl containing water with vinegar. She knelt down in front of him and started to wipe away the blood to discover how bad his wounds were.

He brushed her hand away, 'These cuts are the least of my troubles. I chose unwisely the person to fight with, he is the son of Earl Hervey of Ickworth. He claims I insulted his honour in the heat of the moment and has challenged me to a duel. What am I to do? To preserve the honour of my family I must face him in two days time in Sexton's Meadows, I cannot refuse.'

Phillipa tried to keep calm, suggesting, pleading, 'Cannot your father do something, talk to Lord Hervey, make this stupidity stop before someone gets hurt?'

'I fear he will not intercede on my behalf, he is old fashioned and puts the family's reputation before everything. He will not countenance any show of cowardice or surrender. I will talk to him, though I have little hope he will help me.'

The following day, Sir William returned to the house. He was pale, dishevelled, with panic in his eyes. Phillipa ran to him, flinging her arms around his neck. He needed to say nothing, she knew by his face the Duke had washed his hands of his son's dispute.

Scared, worried for his life, Sir William spent a sleepless night wondering whether he would see another day with his beloved mistress. She did her best to give him confidence and assurance by arguing, 'Most duels normally end with no one harmed, sometimes without a sword being raised in anger.' Her efforts to quell his defeatist mood had little effect. As he left the house, he was quaking with fear. Clutching her tightly the petrified young aristocrat blurted out his undying love in a manner that made Phillipa believe he genuinely feared for his life.

As he walked to Sexton Meadows he met Bartholomew, his younger brother and 'Second' for the duel. As a Second he'd procured the best sabre he could find, sharpened and prepared it. His other responsibility was to ensure the rules of the duel were followed. Seconds were also supposed to try to defuse the argument that led to the duel, by getting an apology from one party or another. Despite his best efforts Bartholomew had failed to defuse Lord Hervey's anger. On hearing this Sir William asked in a bewildered tone, 'How could a simple, drunken argument lead to this fateful encounter, Bartie? I unwittingly besmirched Lord Hervey's reputation and am now about to pay the price, probably with my life.'

Bartie tried to offer words of support to his brother, however, he was aware of Lord Hervey's reputation as a first class swordsman. He, too, feared for Sir William's wellbeing.

An hour later the two men on a grey, miserable morning faced each other, a slight drizzle dampening the duellists and their Seconds. It was obvious this duel would not be settled until blood was drawn—or worse.

Sir William, like all young aristocrats, received swordsmanship lessons as a young man. All part of his education to become a properly equipped gentleman. He never excelled, mainly through lack of purpose and practice. Now he wished he'd paid more attention to his teacher rather than the young maid servants.

The duel commenced at sunrise. Both men unsheathed their sabres. They stood ten paces apart, swatting their blades as they practised parries, lunges and slashes at an imaginary enemy, soon to be replaced by a real one. At the command of the seconds, the duel commenced. The two young aristocrats stopped the posing and circled each other, each seeking an initial advantage. Lord Hervey pounced first with a direct lunge at Sir William's stomach. He parried it easily. He replied with a low slash at his opponents' legs, Lord Hervey jumped back, the blade missing him by a good margin.

Laughing, he mocked, 'you'll have to do better than that young Northumberland. I'd start praying to your God, if I was you.'

After a few minutes, during which Sir William was nicked twice on the sleeve and once, drawing blood, on the leg, he realised his opponent was playing with him. He was a much more accomplished swordsman. One against whom he stood little chance. This was turning into a very one sided contest, the loser probably ending up dead. Fear gripped him. A twist of utter wretchedness grabbed his stomach and for a moment he thought he might void himself, an embarrassment beyond measure.

Sir William tried to concentrate even harder, to anticipate his foe's next move, but a series of feints and lunges exposed his weaknesses, and his body. Lord Hervey nearly ran him through twice, until as he backed away too quickly, he lost his footing. Sir William regained his balance and lunged back, Lord Hervey parried countering with a strong thrust, the sabre's blade cut through his coat, cutting his hip. Barely had he side-stepped, than with lightning speed Lord Hervey, unleashed an unexpected vertical slash causing Sir William to raise his sword to stop his head being split open. In doing so, he lost his balance, slipped on the wet ground and fell backwards onto the thick damp grass. With the speed of a leaping cat, Lord Hervey was standing over him, his sabre pointing downwards pressing hard on Sir William's throat.

His voice a menacing whisper, he leant on his sabre, drawing blood from Sir William's neck, 'Our family motto, Sir William, is —no quarter asked or given—I intend to honour it.' The last thing Sir William remembered before it all went dark was seeing Lord Hervey lift the sabre and someone in the distance shouting, 'Please, stop my Lord....'

...He was in heaven, an angel looking exactly like Phillipa leaning over him, whispering words of relief and encouragement, gently washing his face with a cool, lavender smelling water. He

45

opened his eyes.

'You are awake William, thank the Lord!' Confused, Sir Willam looked around the room, and then up at Phillipa's concerned face, tears of happiness running down her cheeks.

'I...I am alive? How? What happened?' he asked, a perplexed look on his face. 'Why did he not kill me?'

'Obviously, you are alive my dear William, though certainly worse for wear.' He reached up and touched a wound on his cheek, recoiling in pain as he felt the scar. He traced his finger along the cut...he felt the outline of...a letter?

Befuddled, he asked Philippa, 'What is this strange shaped scar...bring me a mirror so I may see the extent of my wounds.'

Phillipa hesitated, 'My Lord apparently Lord Hervey let you live only after the Seconds pleaded for your life. He agreed, but unfortunately, carved the letter "H" on your cheek, with the message I was asked to relay: "let that scar remind you every time you look in the mirror, you are lucky to be alive, courtesy of Lord Hervey."'

He demanded again to look in a mirror. Phillipa reluctantly fetched one and handed it to him. He held it up in front of his disfigured face.

'Oh my Lord Jesus, what an embarrassment. Everyone will know I received this scar from him, I will be a laughing stock. It would have been better if he had killed me.' He closed his eyes trying not to imagine his friend's pitiful looks, the sniggering behind his back, everyone knowing what 'H' stood for. A loser whose honour had been spared only so he could be ridiculed for the rest of his life. He lapsed into silence, despondently wondering how he would recover from the humiliation.

He spent the next two days recuperating. Phillipa fussed around him, regularly cleansing his wounds. The ones she couldn't heal were to his pride and reputation. They would forever be sullied by the scar on his face. Still aching and in pain, he planned to ride back to Barton Hall, confront his father, and discover what the Duke's reaction would be to the ignominy his son had suffered. 'I will return in a day or two my love,' he promised Phillipa, his voice sounded confident, however in his heart, doubts were already troubling him. His Father could be ruthless when it came to the good name of the family.

For days, Phillipa sat staring out of the large front window up and down Whyting Street waiting for his return. After four days, she was worried to the point of not eating and sleeping, convinced something terrible had befallen her lover and benefactor. On the fifth day, there was a knock on the door. A smartly dressed equerry stood there.

With a look of disdain, he handed her a note and a small leather purse. 'This is from Sir William. I will return tomorrow to confirm you have followed the instructions. Good Day to you Miss.'

Phillipa closed the door and sat down at the large refectory table. Her fingers trembling so badly she had difficulty breaking open the wax seal clearly imprinted with the initials 'WN.' The contents were brief and to the point, she recognized Sir William's writing, but not his tone:

My Dear Phillipa,

My father is sending me to our estate near Edinburgh in Scotland. By the time you read this, I will have already left Barton Hall. He has instructed the house in Whyting street be sold with immediate effect. I must ask you therefore to pack your belongings and leave within one day.

I thank you from the bottom of my heart for our time together, but it is now at an end. I hope the money in the enclosed purse will help you start a new life.

Yours affectionately,

William

Phillipa was surprised at how upset she was. She always knew this liaison would be a temporary arrangement, her plan was to leave when she'd saved enough money to buy a cottage in the countryside, and start free from the threat of the workhouse. However, she anticipated it would be on her own terms and at a time of her choosing. Instead the fickle hand of fate meant it was not to be so. Nothing if not philosophical, Phillpia accepted all good things must come to an end.

She peeked inside the leather purse, and smiled. Her dear William had sent a most generous parting present of ten gold sovereigns. Together with her savings, and the gifts she could sell, it totalled more than enough to buy a small farm in the country. With a spring in her step, she packed her bags, money and anything of value she could carry, and left the house before the day's end.

Phillipa turned and looked back as she walked away and smiled, telling herself this house had proved a lucky place to live. She would be sorry to leave it, but a new life of independence now beckoned. As she walked up Whyting Street she had yet to feel the stirrings of a new life within her belly.

Chapter 5

~1523~

'I fear we will be ruined if the King keeps on raising taxes, this will be the third increase in five years,' bemoaned Alderman Stuart Rothschild, as he pored over the accounts of his expenses, trying to find ways to cut costs in his business and household. The house had cost him £90 in 1521, and he spent another £20 in improvements. A fortune he could now ill afford to repay. For a start, his wife, Mary, took to the new fad for putting rugs on the floors, and for privacy, curtains around their bed, even though the servants lived in the south wing. It seemed an unnecessary luxury to his cost conscious thinking. Now she'd ordered a new mattress stuffed with expensive wool and feathers, and, God forbid, replacement oak panelling for the main hall. All of it an extravagance he could bear at the moment. The payments he made to the local money lenders were crippling him as his business struggled to keep pace with a downturn in demand for Suffolk wool. The lender for the purchase of the house was growing impatient to see some of the loan repaid. A man in his position could not default on his debts, it would be catastrophic for his reputation.

He complained out loud again to Mary, 'Why should we pay for the King's excesses? First it was for some grand display for the King of France, now he wants the value of sixth of our estate paid in taxes, it's a huge amount. What next, a half share of all the sheep I sell?'

He looked across the breakfast table at his wife, hoping, but not expecting, some words of support. None were forthcoming, she looked up, pale and listless. He added, provocatively, 'We may have to sell the house, Mary.'

Expressionless, she looked up, then half heartedly suggested, 'Well, we could let one of the maids go? Would that help?'

'I think we need to do more than that, but it's a start. Who do you have in mind?'

'I would suggest Anne, she is lazy and rude. I have been looking for an excuse to get rid of her.'

Stuart tried to hide his dismay. Anne might be lazy and rude, but she was willing and able in other matters, ones he would miss if she left. For six months they had indulged in some exhausting bedroom dalliances when his wife went to visit relatives in Long Melford. Half his age, barely out of her teen years, she was an exciting and insatiable lover, making up for an aspect of his marriage that had long since faded. After five children, of which only three had reached puberty, his wife's desires in that department had waned considerably. Indeed, in

51

the months since the death of their last child at birth, she was beset with a melancholy that would not leave her.

Young Anne was an enjoyable substitute, he couldn't let her be sacked. He casually backpedalled.

'Let's not be too hasty in getting rid of any staff. I'll keep working on these figures to see if I can't find other ways to save a little money. In your delicate state my dear I want you to have no extra concerns about running the house.'

As he rose from the table, collecting up his papers, there was a thunderous banging on the front door. Without waiting to be invited in, his next door neighbour burst into the hallway. 'Alderman, Alderman, you must come quickly, there is a riot in the town square.'

His neighbour, Joshua Le Mesurer was wild eyed with terror as he described what he'd witnessed. 'It's terrifying Alderman, there must be two or three hundred of them, mainly peasants, complaining about the latest taxes. They are getting frustrated and violent that no one is listening to them. Someone has gone to fetch the Duke to see if he can bring some armed men to calm them down. I fear it will get out of control before he arrives.'

Stuart turned to his wife, 'Mary, you stay here and lock the door, I must go and see if I can stop this foolhardiness. Joshua, let us make haste'

Joshua hesitated, 'I would urge caution, Alderman, some would see you as the enemy, being a representative of the King in these parts.'

'I understand your concern, but I must try something before it gets out of hand,' he grabbed his cloak and hat as he rushed down the hallway out into the street, slamming the door behind him.

As they reached the top of Whyting street and turned into the Buttermarket, they could hear a cacophony of shouts and yelling as the crowd vented their ire at anyone who would listen. Suddenly, there was a loud cheer as a cart of wool was set on fire, then a second. A particularly dangerous act when all the houses around them were made of timber.

The Alderman looked at the chaotic scene in front of him, 'Joshua, I have to try and calm them down, somehow. There will be injuries and worse if I don't.'

'But how? They are beyond reasoning, I fear. Arguing with them could be dangerous. Plus, you are unarmed Alderman, please take my dagger, at least. It will give you some protection.'

'Thank you Joshua, but no, I don't want to antagonise them any further. But I do need to get their attention….'

He looked around, his eyes coming to rest on a horse and small cart tied up close by. An idea sprang to mind. Possibly foolhardy, though under the circumstances the Alderman saw no alternative.

'Joshua, would you help me drive that cart into the crowd, but slowly, we must go carefully.'

For a moment Joshua looked petrified at the prospect of wading into a rioting mob. He was a big man, imposing and not easily intimidated, however, this, this was lunacy.

'Joshua?' The Alderman had to shout to make himself heard, 'Are you with me? I need your help. Now. We must move without delay.'

Reluctantly, he agreed, 'Yes, yes, Alderman, I am with you.'

They quickly untied the horse and Joshua climbed up onto the seat and flicked the reins to get the animal moving and heading towards the crowd, who were still noisily cheering the burning carts. The poor brute was at first unwilling to approach the noise and fire, but with some not so gentle persuasion, it walked nervously forward into the noisy throng.

The Alderman stood up on the back of the cart. He tried not to show his fear. As an appointee by the King, he was there to ensure the monarch's laws were obeyed. This was the first time he'd confronted his townsfolk hell bent on breaking them. But it was vital to his reputation that he stood up to this braying mob. Calming his nerves and quivering voice, he cupped his hands around his mouth and bellowed with such force he felt his throat straining.

'GENTLEMEN! Please, please listen to me!' After shouting this a few times, and with help from an emboldened Joshua, who also belted out some loud demands for quiet, the crowd slowly settled down. The Alderman was unknown to some of the rioters, so he introduced himself, aware that any association with the King could put him in peril with this riled up mob.

'I am Alderman Stuart Rothschild. I know a few of you here today. I know you are good, law-abiding people. I speak to you as a fellow resident of Bury St Edmunds, not in my office as one of the King's representatives. I am imploring you; please, please stop this nuisance at once. You are all in danger of being imprisoned as traitors if you continue to protest against the King. I understand your frustration against these new taxes, but it is the law and must be obeyed.'

'Alright for you to say!' shouted one protester, close to the cart. 'Easy for your type, what with your fancy clothes and big houses. You can afford to put food on your table. If we have to pay these extra taxes our families will starve!' Cheers of agreement greeted his words.

A young woman, a baby perched on her hip, screamed her own insult, 'You people are all the same! Suckling off the King's tit. Growing fat while we starve, telling us to keep quiet. A plague on you and your household!' The crowd agreed and cheered even louder at her accusation. The heckling increased, and for a moment, the Alderman feared he was fighting a losing battle trying to quell their pent up fury.

Suddenly, he felt something hit his head, then on his chest. He looked down to see a large blotch of red staining his coat. Thankfully only a rotten tomato. He reached up to his head, he looked at his hand, now yellow with egg yolk. More followed. The crowd jeered, encouraging more projectiles to rain down on him. For a second, the Alderman was tempted to jump down from the cart and take cover. Then a feeling of anger roused his courage and he stood still and straight, looking directly into the crowd. The crowd, seeing his determination not to be cowed by their actions, slowly stopped the hail of rotten food.

He raised his hands in supplication, a gesture he hoped would calm the fraught atmosphere, 'People of Bury St Edmunds, I know, I understand, we are all finding things difficult at this time. Rich and poor. But rioting, and being hanged won't solve your problems. Please go back to your homes before the Duke and his men arrive. They will show no mercy in enforcing the King's will. I am begging you for you and your family's sake, go home now!'

The Alderman's words swayed a few in the crowd, who made moves to leave. Unfortunately, most wanted to take the fight, their grievances, down to the Abbey. A symbol of the wealth and excesses they found so upsetting. One firebrand, who the Alderman recognized as John Davy shouted, 'Let's go see that thieving bloodsucker, the Abbot. I hear he has food to feed an army. 'Bout time he shared it with all of us, eh?' He turned round to the crowd, waving his arms above his head, shouting, 'Who's with me?' Most of the rioters clamoured in agreement and waving clubs and pitchforks in the air, swiftly moved past the Alderman and Joshua's cart heading down Abbeygate street towards the Abbey gates.

Frustrated at his failure to break up the riot, the Alderman turned to Joshua, 'What are we to do now? They probably have closed the Abbey Gate already, and that will only annoy this rabble even more. I fear this will all end badly.'

Joshua, shrugged his shoulders, 'Until they find another way in. The Abbey isn't a castle, they will gain entry somehow, then Lord help the Abbot and the Monks. Shall we follow them?'

The Alderman paused for a moment, the rabble already disappearing down the hill towards their destination, 'I fear if we do, we will witness something terrible, they are in no mood for compromise...but, yes, let us see how events develop, maybe we will have another chance to dissuade them from doing anything they will regret.'

'I applaud your optimism Alderman, however I feel it may be misplaced. They are in no mood to compromise. Let us make haste to see what transpires.'

The two men jumped down from the cart and hurried across the Buttermarket following the noisy protestors. As they passed the two burnt out hay carts the Alderman muttered a quick prayer of thanks that no buildings had caught fire. At least that was something to thank the Lord for. People who had taken refuge in shops and inns were now emerging, milling around, inspecting the damage and excitedly discussing the riot they just witnessed. Many decided to follow the mob down to the Abbey to see how events unfolded. A few thanked the Alderman and Joshua for their efforts at quelling the mob, most said nothing, secretly in agreement with their protests.

As the two men ran down towards the Abbey's Gate, they stopped at the edge of Angel Hill, the large square in front of the Abbey. From their vantage point they could see the protestors hacking away at the huge, solid oak doors. They were a formidable barrier, the rioter's efforts at breaking them down were proving futile. pitchforks and spades made little impact on the six inch thick solid oak doors. Enraged at their inability to break through them, John Davy shouted something the two men couldn't hear and then saw the crowd turn towards the East Gate of the town where the Abbey's wall crossed the River Lark, affording an easier point of entry.

Suddenly, from Northgate street appeared twenty mounted men, swords drawn. They galloped straight for the group of rioters, the thundering noise of the horses hooves and shouts of the men on horseback halted their progress. Surprise and fear crossed their faces as they saw the horsemen, swords drawn, bearing down on them.

'Is that the Duke? Thank God! He has arrived just in time!' shouted Joshua, relief in his voice.

The Alderman, straining his eyes, replied, 'I do not think so. Ah! I recognize the coat of arms, it is Sir Robert Drury from Hawstead. That is good news, he is a reasonable man, let us hope he can resolve this without any violence. I am sure if it had been the Duke, blood would have been spilled.'

As he finished speaking, the horseman started to encircle the protestors and corral them into the corner of Angel Hill. Sir Robert rode up to the now silent rabble. He looked down, his sword pointing directly at them. Now he had their attention, he gave them two stark choices: 'You are breaking the law, no matter how well founded your grievances. You insult our King with your protests and also threaten to damage Holy property. If you persist, I will imprison all of you and see you hanged before the month's end. Or, you can leave peaceably, go to your homes and I will forget your treasonous actions. But be warned, should I ever have cause to come here again to deal with such lawbreaking, I swear you will feel the point of this sword in your belly. What is it to be?'

Cornered, faced with a force of knights on horseback, and the threat of execution, quickly persuaded the now silent protestors that discretion was the better part of valour. Dejectedly, they started to leave, their bravado evaporating, leaving only an abiding sense of frustration. Even the verbose John Davy left with his head bowed, now at a loss for words. Within minutes, the square was empty.

Joshua laughed, turning to the Alderman he exclaimed, 'Ha! They're all piss and wind. Look at them cowering like so many beaten dogs. They are a sorry sight indeed. Lucky the gallows don't have their names on them this time.'

'You are right Joshua, but their concerns are justified. These new taxes will be the ruin of rich and poor. They have nothing to lose, which makes them dangerous and unpredictable. I fear today will not be the last time we see such troubles.'

The Alderman was right. The riot in Bury St Edmunds was repeated across the county. The town of Lavenham twelve miles south of Bury saw a large-scale protest numbering four thousand people. The intervention of local aristocrats, Thomas Spring and Sir Thomas Jermyne of Rushbroke, helped contain the troubles before they spread to neighbouring towns. Innovatively in Lavenham, Thomas Spring had all the church bells removed, thereby preventing them being used as a call to arms by the troublemakers.

Still shaken from the morning's upsetting events, the Alderman agreed with Joshua a glass of ale would be most welcome. They walked across from Pulter's Rowe in front of the Abbey to Churchgate street and entered the White Swan Inn.

Normally men of the Alderman's standing would not enter such establishments. They were places of refuge for the poor and homeless as well as places to drink and eat. Gambling, whoring and drunkenness were all part of the entertainment to be found there. The company was not the most salubrious, explained Joshua, but the ale in this establishment 'was excellent, the best in Bury.

Ignoring the looks from other drinker's at the Alderman's food stained attire, they settled with two tankards of the frothy warm drink to discuss the riot, and the reasons behind it.

Joshua was full of praise for the Alderman's attempts to quell the riot. 'You deserve a drink, you did an exceptional job there today Stuart. That could have turned out a lot worse if it wasn't for your brave words. I hope the King gets to hear about it.'

'Thank you Joshua, treasonous though it might sound—I do have some sympathy for their plight. Since the new King was crowned in 1509, the taxes have increased so many times, you cannot blame the poor for their actions. I am likewise feeling squeezed by this latest tax, when will it end? How are you faring?'

'Like you, Alderman, times are difficult for me too. Not just the King's taxes, but the Abbey continues to take money from the inhabitants of the town, charging fees, levying fines for the most petty things. I have been told many of the rich are now leaving money to the town for improving the roads and buildings, not the Abbey. I intend to do the same. They are vultures, I will leave them no scraps in my will. Assuming I have any money left when I die!'

The Alderman took a swig of ale, and wiped his mouth with the sleeve of his shirt. 'Indeed I feel the same. The cost of my new house is crippling me, the lenders keep charging more interest and my wife spends money like water. Ever since we moved there we seem to have had bad luck. Losing two of my dear children at birth, my business is struggling and my wife ails with some malady no physician or apothecary can identify.'

The men continued to commiserate with each other, drinking more ale than they realised. By mid-afternoon, a little worse for wear, they stumbled out of the inn and walked up Westgate Street. On the left were the water meadows known as the Butts where once compulsory Archery practice took place. The men erratically made their way up Whyting street.

At the Alderman's house they shook hands, congratulating each other on a pleasant end to a nerve wracking day. He went inside to relay the extraordinary events to Mary. As he entered the hall he was shocked to see his wife and the maid Anne sitting side by side at the dining table. Mary looked stern while Anne wept uncontrollably.

The Alderman's heart sank, had Mary decided to sack the housemaid after all?

He walked up to the table, suddenly sober, and asked, 'What in God's name is the matter, what has happened?'

Mary looked at him with disgust in her eyes, 'Oh yes, Stuart something has happened alright,' she turned to Anne. 'Tell him, you little whore.'

Through red, tear filled eyes she blubbered, 'Sire...master, I am with child. The baby is yours.'

Chapter 6

The kitchen was a hot, humid cauldron of activity from before dawn. Head cook Jean Browning was preparing dinner for noon. Alderman Stuart was entertaining some local businessmen and the meal had to impress. One of the kitchen maids was lugging in pails of water from the well outside the back door. Another was preparing the vegetables: onions and cabbages. While the third was cutting up half a small boar and a haunch of venison. All obtained from the local market in Bury the day before. Little was stored, it was all bought fresh, as and when needed.

Jean was checking on the bread that had been in the oven for nearly an hour. She pulled open the wooden door, dislodging the thin strips of hardened dough that had been used to seal the cracks between the door and the brick surround. The heat swept out across her face. Wiping the perspiration off her with a cloth, she peered inside, announcing, 'Perfect! Loaves fit for a King! Anne, take these out and put them on the high shelf, out of the way of hungry hands.'

Anne, now heavily pregnant, waddled over to take them. She had been relegated to menial kitchen duties after the revelations of her affair with the Alderman. Jean added, 'Then when you've done that, go into the great hall, keep the fire stoked and those pots of hot water ready for the vegetables and meat.'

The kitchen was large but with several servants at work, a large central preparation table, and cupboards all around the walls, space was, at times, limited. Anne did as beckoned and walked into the great hall where a huge fireplace not just heated the room, but cooked the food as well. There was no chimney, the smoke drifted up to a hole in the ceiling to escape. It was not an efficient way to extract the smoke, so the room always had a burnt haze and smell, even with the windows and shutters open. Anne checked all the candles were lit and replenished those nearly burnt to the holders.

Standing by the fire, staring into the roaring flames, Anne still seethed at her fall from grace in the Alderman's household. Her affair with him had not gone to plan. He promised she would become his mistress, give her a cottage on Risbygate street for her own use, with a modest annual allowance. Becoming pregnant had ruined those plans. Now she was to stay in the house, doing menial duties until the baby arrived, then, who knew?

The church frowned on adultery and unmarried mothers. The Alderman, because of his position, would probably give the Abbot a handsome donation and be absolved of his sins. As for Anne? Her future was uncertain, but unlikely to be pleasant. If she was thrown out of the house, to become a vagrant or beggar it would mean being whipped or beaten until she left the town and returned to her home village of Nowton and thrown into the Workhouse. For weeks her mind whirled with thoughts of revenge. Would anyone believe her if she claimed the Alderman had forced himself on her? Would he take her as his wife if Mary's illness was to worsen, possibly causing her death? Or had an accident? Could she somehow blackmail him with the rape accusation? Should she get rid of the baby and say he forced her to do so?

She decided to confront the Alderman, who'd ignored her since she revealed her pregnancy, and the affair had become public, at least within the household. She left the fire and went upstairs to his room. As she neared the door, raised voices stopped her from knocking. Whatever the argument was between the couple, now was not the time to interrupt. Frustrated, she crept back downstairs, not before stopping to straighten a large rug at the top of the stairs. Within minutes, she was back in front of the fire, no one the wiser for her temporary absence.

Back in the kitchen, one of the maids, busy chopping up a pile of onions, turned to Jean, 'I hear some of the grand homes have things called chimneys now to get rid of the smoke from the fire. Means they can cook in the kitchen. Wonder if Master Stuart might do that sometime?'

Jean looked bemused, 'A chimney? Never heard of such a thing I'm sure. Well that's something we'll have to deal with when the master feels fit to make any changes. Now, stop your daydreaming and go help Davy in the Buttery preparing the drinks. Tell him to get the best red wine out, it's a special occasion.'

Suddenly, the door to the kitchen burst open and Catherine, Mary's personal maid rushed in, panic in her voice, 'Someone go and get the physician! Mistress Mary has fallen down the stairs and hit her head in a bad way on the steps. Bring some hot water and a cloth at once. Hurry, hurry! With that, she fled back across the great hall, passing an unconcerned Anne still tending the fire. She seemed in no hurry to help. Catherine barely glanced at her as she ran back to aid her mistress.

She found the Alderman seated on the stairs cradling his wife's head in his lap, desperately trying to stem the flow of blood from the wound. He looked up, distraught, as Catherine returned, quickly followed by Jean and the scullery boy, Davy, with a pail of hot water.

The Alderman, his voice quivering with desperation, asked, 'Has the physician been called? Her breathing is very weak, I cannot stop the blood. Can you do anything to help Catherine? Please do something, please.'

'Master, can you carry her to your bed to make her more comfortable?' The Alderman nodded and did as Catherine requested, nearly tripping over a loosened rug at the top of the stairs as he carried the unconscious body of his wife to the bedroom.

It took an hour for the physician to arrive. He could do little. 'There is no point in bleeding her, she has already lost so much blood. Her heartbeat is irregular, she is very weak. All I can suggest is to bind her head tightly with cloth and keep her comfortable. She is in the good Lord's hands now, we must all pray for her recovery.'

As the physician left, he was accosted by Anne at the front door, away from anyone else in the household. Their conversation was brief. A piece of paper exchanged hands and he quickly walked off down Whyting street, shaking his head in disapproval.

For the next three days, the Alderman never left his wife's side. He prayed incessantly for her recovery. He sent for the Abbot who spent an hour praying with him at her bedside. The Alderman's three children were bereft with concern, not venturing outside, spending hours beside their ailing mother, holding her hand and silently beseeching her to open her eyes.

The household staff moved silently around the house counting prayers on their rosaries. Everyone was visibly upset, except Anne who seemed indifferent to the melancholy atmosphere pervading the house. By the fourth day, Mary showed no sign of improvement. When it was obvious she was fading fast, a priest was summoned to perform the Last Rites. The family knelt around her bed praying for her soul, waiting for the inevitable. On the evening of the fourth day after her accident, Mary died of a brain haemorrhage.

*****

'Father, father,' the Alderman's teenage son's voice echoed up the stairs to his study.

Not deigning to respond to a shouted demand from the other side of the house, he waited until his breathless son careered into the room, 'Yes Francis, how can I help you?'

'There's about to be an execution, a burning at the stake of some witch. Can we go and watch…please?' begged the boy.

The Alderman was aware an unfortunate soul was due to meet her fate, but not on this day. He hesitated, burning at the stake was a ghastly, painful and gruesome way to die. Furthermore, he knew from previous such executions, it wasn't pleasant for the crowd either, the screams, the smell of burning flesh. Quite why anyone found this entertaining left him bemused. However, it was supposed to be a deterrent, an education that breaking the law could have dreadful consequences. Was it too soon for a thirteen-year-old to witness such a macabre spectacle? If only Mary was here, she would have known what to do. But, alas, such decisions were now his to make alone.

He looked sternly at his son, 'Francis, you know watching someone burn to death is neither sport nor a cause for celebration. No matter how guilty the person is of the crime they've committed it is a ghastly way to die. I will come with you and you will be on your best behaviour. You understand all of what I have said?'

Francis was too excited to say anything except agree with his Father's warning. They left the house and walked up Whyting street, across the, now empty, large square where the twice weekly markets took place. Then down Little Brakelonde and into Northgate Street. There they joined a stream of people walking to the site of public executions at Henhow on Thingoe Hill, just outside the North gate of the town.

By the time the Alderman and his son arrived at the execution site, a crowd of several hundred were there. Food and Ale sellers were doing a brisk trade. The atmosphere was almost festive, despite the grim reason they were all there. Fruit and vegetable sellers brought rotten produce for the spectators to throw at the victim. They waited for nearly an hour before cheers and cat calls announced the arrival of the prisoner. They turned to see a cart being pulled by an oxen trundle towards them carrying the victim. She was a middle aged woman, long scraggly grey hair, the remnants of her clothes barely covering her emaciated body. The crowd threw not just insults, but the rancid fruit, and vegetables too. Others found rocks and lumps of mud to hurl, in fact anything to make sure the victim's last minutes were as unpleasant as possible.

As she approached her place of execution, the woman stood head bowed, resignedly accepting her fate and the final indignities she was suffering. She was bound hand and foot with a rope around her neck. The Alderman hoped the executioner would spare her being burnt alive and strangle her just as the faggotts were lit—an increasingly common practice.

The victim was dragged off the cart and manhandled to the post. The executioner waited for her to say any words of repentance. The crowd hushed. This was an integral part of the process and people came to hear the guilty's final words, of equal importance as the manner with which they conducted themselves in their final moments on this earth. Frequently, a brave demeanour and some conciliatory words of regret and prayer would ensure they had a *good execution*, one that was swift and as far as possible, painless.

The woman looked up at the expectant crowd and said in a surprisingly strong voice, 'I come here, accepting my punishment, but not my guilt. As God is my witness, I have always been a devout Catholic, and believed in God's mercy and forgiveness. He may have deserted me in my final hours, but my faith is still strong. These charges against me of witchcraft are false and evil. I know when I am consumed by these flames, my soul will still go to meet my God in heaven. For those that have accused me, your body may never be eaten by flames, but as God is my witness, your soul will be. May God have mercy on you all.'

The crowd were awed to silence by her heartfelt words.

With those words, she bowed her head in prayer while the executioner piled up the faggotts around her feet as high as her waist, then lit them. As the smoke rose and flames took hold, the Alderman was relieved to see the executioner run behind the post to which the victim had been tied and hastily turn the rope around her neck until she passed out, or died—he hoped, the latter.

While they may have been spared the victim's screams of pain, not so the smell as the flames consumed her flesh. It was sickly, sweet and vomit inducing, soon most of the crowd were covering their mouths and quickly leaving. The Alderman looked at his son to see his reaction. He was shocked and very pale, tears in his eyes. Lesson learnt, he hoped. 'Seen enough? Shall we go home now?'

Francis nodded in silent agreement.

Nothing was said until they reached their house. Finally, the Alderman asked his son, 'So Francis, what did you make of that? Witnessing your first execution?'

Putting on a brave face, he answered, 'It was interesting, Father. I do believe she may have been innocent, what say you?"

Noncommittally he replied, 'I don't know Francis, I don't know. But it matters little now, she is dead. Let us go in and say a short prayer for her. Then, I believe, you have some studies to complete?'

As they entered the great hall of the house, they could hear screams of agony coming from the servant's quarters. The Alderman ran into the kitchen on the ground floor and up the stairs to where the servants slept, the screams growing longer and louder. Three servants were peering through a door from whence the screams emanated.

'What is happening?' The Alderman demanded, elbowing his way past them. He entered to see Anne writhing on the bed, below the waist her clothes were covered in blood. Catherine was wiping Anne's feverish face trying to comfort and ease her distress. Again the Alderman asked, 'Just what is happening to her? Does anyone know?'

Catherine looked up, answering, 'She has lost the baby, Sire. Now, we have to try and save her, she has bled a considerable amount. It may be too late to get a physician. I have seen this happen before, when a baby arrives early, the next few hours will tell us if the Lord desires she live.'

71

The Alderman indicated he wished to talk to Catherine privately. Down in the great hall away from the other servants, he asked what might have caused Anne to lose the baby?

'As God is my witness, I do not know Sire. She did say she spoke to a physician about obtaining some herbs to end the pregnancy. But I do not believe she ever took anything. I think it is just bad luck or God's will. Poor girl this may kill her...also the baby was...well not quite proper, Sire."

'What do you mean "not quite proper?"'

Catherine hesitantly explained that the baby was slightly deformed, 'He seemingly had no eyes Sire, maybe it was for the best he didn't...survive?'

Speechless for a moment, the Alderman, visibly upset, shook his head in sorrow, 'That is terrible indeed, maybe you are right Catherine. God works in mysterious ways it seems.' Nevertheless, while he was saddened at the death of the child and Anne's distress, in a small way, he was relieved at this awful news.

The Alderman dismissed her with instructions to do all she could to save Anne. He may not have loved the girl, but he was very fond of her, and certainly missed their intimate company. He went disconsolately up to his study. However, he found it impossible to work. He cast his mind back to the rumours he heard of a previous owner having the house blessed to rid it of some evil spells. He didn't believe in such things, of course. Though it did cross his mind, the loss of Anne's baby, together with his wife's death and before that his last two children, dying before they lived to utter a single breath, would be enough to make many believe this house was one which harboured bad luck.

To compound his suspicions, two days later Anne died. He remained at the house, unhappy and lonely for many more years before selling when his creditor's patience finally ran out.

Chapter 7

~1533~

Sir Reginald Willoughby walked around his new house recently bought from the destitute Alderman, whose business had finally failed him the previous year. In a final effort to stave off his creditors, the Alderman sold off many of the valuable pieces of furniture and fittings. Inside, the house was now bare, devoid of any luxury or refinement. It was in a sorry state of repair too, and would need a lot of money to bring it up to his high standards. Despite its dismal condition, Sir Reginald was delighted to have acquired such a large house in a prestigious part of the town.

Sir Reginald, a successful land and property investor, owned several houses in the town. He was keen to buy one in Whyting street as the area was demolishing the very old small houses, many built soon after the grid had been laid out in 1080. Gradually, in their place were built handsome new double gabled houses like the one he had just bought for a modest £85.

Among the improvements he intended to make was the building of a chimney in the great hall, a more efficient way of ridding the room of smoke than a hole in the roof. It would ensure a cleaner atmosphere, and the ability to build a second storey connecting the two wings of the house. He would also install glass in all the windows. Winter was approaching and this would help keep the house much warmer.

Sir Reginald, was a widower, his wife having succumbed to a mystery illness some three years ago. He hoped to find a new, younger wife to fill the house with children. At his age, 42, with his wealth and a luxurious home near the centre of Bury, he felt sure he would soon attract a fine lady. Tall, slim with a slight limp from a horse riding accident, he cut an imposing figure. His grey beard was neatly trimmed, his wrinkle free face making him look younger than his age. He considered himself an eligible catch.

As he walked around the empty house rattling off notes on the building work he wanted done to his assistant, there was a knock at the door. He had yet to employ any servants, so he asked Paul to ascertain who wished to see him.

He quickly returned, 'It is a Prior Cooper, one of the Abbey's stewards. He says he has a business proposition for you. He declined to go into detail with me.'

While it was most unusual to have a visitor of such stature arrive unannounced, Sir Reginald was intrigued by the reason for the Prior's visit. 'Very well, show him in, I will be upstairs in my study.'

A minute later, the Prior entered Sir Reginald's sparsely furnished room, 'I apologise for the lack of comforts, I only purchased the property a few weeks ago and have yet to furnish it.' Of course the man surely knew of the recent sale. He paid the Abbey a fee for the pleasure of allowing him to make the transaction. The Abbey's financial tentacles touched every part of the town's private and business dealings.

'Please do not apologise Sir, my visit is unexpected, I appreciate you seeing me at such short notice. However, I think you will find what I have to say to your benefit.'

'It is a pleasure to meet you. Your words intrigue me, Prior, please explain further.'

'Firstly, can you assure me this conversation will remain completely private? It is of an extremely delicate nature.'

Sir Reginald confirmed that would be the case then waited to see what this mysterious matter was all about.

Conspiratorially he whispered, 'I should add, if news of this meeting becomes public before our dealings are complete it could be not just costly, but dangerous as well.' Without waiting for a reaction, the Prior continued.

'As you may be aware, the finances of the Abbey are, well how can I put this, in a perilous state. Income from taxes, rent and farming are down, these are difficult times even for an organisation as large as the Abbey.

'Therefore, the Abbot has asked me to discreetly talk to successful land owners such as yourself about the sale of large areas of its landholdings. For obvious reasons, if this becomes public before any transactions are completed, it could result in values increasing. That said, the prices at which we are willing to divest the properties are much below their worth, and should over a period of time prove to be an excellent investment.'

He was surprised to hear the Abbey was in such financial straits. Keeping that thought to himself, noncommittally Sir Reginald agreed, 'Well we are all suffering a decline in revenues Prior. That said, these properties you are willing to sell, can you be more precise as to their whereabouts, size and price?'

The Prior pulled out a roll of paper and opened it on the desk, 'This lists the properties currently for divestment. More may become available next year. Would you care to look now? I cannot leave this list with you. I am happy to wait while you peruse it.'

Sir Reginald ran his eyes down the list. He counted twenty properties. Everything from houses in Bury St Edmunds, to estates as far afield as Ipswich, Thetford, Newmarket and Lavenham. Some were small farms of just a few acres, others spanned several hundred. Two immediately caught his eye. Both adjoined land he already owned, and would conveniently expand his current holdings by a considerable size. Controlling his excitement Sir Angus took his time studying the whole list in detail before replying.

'Interesting Prior, these are some fine properties. Subject to me visiting and inspecting them I would provisionally put my name next to the ones near Long Melford and Lavenham. Based on your figures that is a total of 850 acres and a sum of £150?'

'Indeed Sir Reginald, excellent and very logical choices, bearing in mind your existing holdings. I can give you two weeks to contact me again with a firm offer, or I will make them available to others I am visiting over the next few days.'

'Two weeks? That is a short deadline for such a large transaction. I will have to borrow some of the purchase price, I will contact my lenders immediately. However, they work slowly.'

The Prior became a little more forceful, 'I understand that Sir Reginald but I have a short deadline within which to work. I hope you can accommodate it. Before I go, is this the house that was exorcized by the Abbot Rattlesden some decades ago? I was perusing old Abbey records and came across a note left by him to that effect?'

Sir Reginald, his attention still on the maps and paperwork in front of him, grunted a rebuttal, 'I know nothing of the history of this house Prior, why do you ask?

The Prior pointed up to one of the large oak beams supporting the ceiling. 'See, those marks, the swirls and upturned crosses. They were, indeed still are, signs of the devil. I don't wish to alarm you but you may want to get them replaced, they could indicate some spell or curse has been placed upon this house.'

Laughing, Sir Reginald replied, 'I doubt that very much, Prior. Surely as a man of the cloth you do not believe in such hocus pocus?'

'Sir, as a firm believer in the power of good and God, I have to accept there is evil too in this world in the guise of Satan. His disciples in the form of witches and wizards can create powerful and long lasting spells of great power.' He made an elaborate sign of the cross, then fell silent, he didn't want to distract his potential purchaser from the business at hand.

The Prior waited a few minutes then asked, 'Sir Reginald, will you be able to meet my deadline. I hope you can accommodate it. These are likely to be popular properties among the other buyers I am due to visit.'

Becoming irritated at the Prior's badgering, he replied curtly, "I will be ready to sign the documents in two weeks.'

Satisfied, the Prior stood up to leave, extending his hand. As Sir Reginald shook it, he repeated the need for secrecy, a strange request for such a large amount of land from a well known landowner. The Abbey was always buying and selling properties, why the persistent demand for this all to be done in such a clandestine manner? If he had suspicions, they were allayed by the tempting price of the properties and the future profits he could derive from them. After the Prior left, Sir Reginald called his assistant and asked him to make plans for a trip to Sudbury and Lavenham. Time was of the essence. Meanwhile, he would visit some money lenders to see what their rates would be for the substantial sum he needed to raise.

Lavenham and Sudbury are to the south east of Bury St Edmunds, but a few hours away. Sir Reginald and Paul left the town two days later to inspect the properties. The rolling Suffolk countryside was displaying its stunning palette of autumn colours, the golds, reds and yellows of the leaves contrasted against a clear blue sky. It was a beautiful day for a ride. They made their way to the first landholding on the list, 410 acres north of the wealthy town of Lavenham, which included the hamlet of Rooksey Green. The land was mostly arable, though the crops had now been harvested. It looked fertile and well kept, thought Sir Reginald.

Which was more than could be said for the hamlet itself. The twenty or thirty cottages were in poor repair, thatch roofs were sagging and rotten, the houses in desperate need of maintenance. They stopped at the small church and sought out the parish priest. They found him dispensing confession, a queue of impoverished churchgoers, sitting patiently waiting their turn on the church pews.

Hearing the door slam, the priest came out of the confessional to greet them. His robes were dirty and torn. His worn and tired round face held kindly eyes and a gentle smile. He walked up and introduced himself, 'I am Father Richard Smith, welcome to our humble church. How may I help you gentleman today?'

'Good day Father, I am Sir Reginald Willoughby and this is my assistant Paul.' Deciding to bend the truth so as to avoid the real reason for their visit, he explained, 'I am here on behalf of the Abbey who have offered me the chance to lease the land around here from them. I am surveying it to see exactly what assets might be included, and its income potential, so as to value it more accurately.'

Moving away from the parishioners, the priest took them outside. With a sweep of his arm to indicate the extent of the tiny hamlet, he said, 'Well, this is all that we have Sir Reginald, and as you see, a sorry state it is in, if I am to be honest. The Abbey has failed in recent years to complete any repairs to the houses, barns, walls, indeed even my church. The land is fertile and the people work hard and produce ample crops, but they demand more and more from us in rent and tithe, then always claim they have no money for upkeep of the hamlet. We are in a sad state of affairs and have been for many years. I have pleaded for their help on numerous occasions but without success....'

The priest stopped talking, fearing he may have spoken out of turn. It didn't pay to criticise the Abbot, he wielded immense power over most of the population, priests in particular. His church may be impoverished, but it was a roof over his head, one that could be quickly removed at the Abbot's behest.

The priest is stating the obvious, thought Sir Reginald, however, did he detect something more the priest wished to say? The Abbey was renowned for its miserliness and indifference towards its tenants, only caring for the income they produced. To purchase this land would be just the initial cost, repairing the houses and equipment a lot more. He turned to Paul, 'Take a look round at the buildings, list what repairs need doing so we can estimate the costs.' Paul nodded. Sir Reginald walked off with the priest, down the muddy track which separated the two rows of houses in the hamlet.

'Father, now it is just the two of us, you can speak freely. I urge you to be forthright with me if I am to become your landlord. I need to know what troubles might befall me if I take over this land.'

The priest hesitated before saying anything. Speaking ill of the Abbey was a dangerous pastime. 'You have to understand Sir, what I am about to tell you could cause my death if the Abbot discovered it is I who have revealed these sordid activities....'

'You have my oath Father, this will go no further...please speak your mind. You say, "sordid activities." Exactly what are you inferring?'

The priest continued walking, hands clasped behind his back, composing his thoughts for a few moments.

'I know not when this started, certainly before I arrived here three years ago. It happens but once or twice a year. A Prior and some guards from the Abbey appear, and demand everyone meet in the church. They look for any girls and boys who have reached puberty since their last visit and without asking their parents, take them. They say for induction into the priesthood or for girls to become nuns. But we never see or hear from them again. I have been to the Abbey myself to seek them out but no one claims to know anything about their whereabouts. I have my suspicions as to their fate, but cannot find out more to confirm it.'

Sir Reginald, stopped walking and faced the priest directly, 'These are dangerous accusations Father. You are telling me the Abbey is abducting these children, if not to become priests or nuns, then what?'

The priest didn't look at Sir Reginald, his eyes remained fixed to the ground, 'Sire, I have no certain proof what I am about to say is the truth. I have heard they may be used for...for appeasing the carnal desires of the monks and nuns....'

The knight took a step back mortified at these disgusting allegations, 'What? Father, these accusations are outrageous, even heretical. Have you any proof that these lecherous activities are taking place? Why do you assume the worst possible outcome for your young people's disappearance?'

'Because a parent from the next village rescued one of his daughters from the Priory at Thetford, and she claimed such licentiousness was inflicted upon her. By her account, it was both the nuns and the monks that used her until she was no longer needed. That is all I know. Sir Reginald, our hamlet is dying because many strong young men and women are being abducted, leaving us without enough hands to work the land. Soon, it will be a place of old men and women where little physical work can be done.'

Sir Reginald, had difficulty digesting these horrendous accusations, let alone the implications for his potential purchase of the land. Did he really want to find himself in the middle of some sordid legal battle if this ever became public? Or if he did complete the purchase, would he have to stop such abductions— and at what cost? Plus, not just from the moral standpoint, but the purely practical one: if no one was able to work the land, his investment would become worthless in years to come.

Of course he had heard that the Abbey, and other holy places like it, were not always havens of prayer and holiness. He was led to believe such activities took place between nuns and monks only. Could they really be using young people to satisfy such urges? He found it impossible to believe. Why hadn't some of them complained?

'Father, why have you not reported it to the Justice of the Peace, or even the Ecclesiastical Church Court?'

'Sire, if the Abbey heard such accusations being made by us, we would be evicted. They have control over our lives and livelihood. We have little choice but to bite our tongues.'

Sir Reginald, chose his words carefully, 'If what you say is true Father, these are indeed dire acts that must be stopped. Much as I would like to help, I need to think these matters over before I do anything. Becoming landlord of this property would find me having to take action against the Abbey. That I cannot do without more proof. You have my sympathies. These are terrible acts being committed against innocent children. It is a dreadful misfortune for you and your parishioners. Let me decide what I intend to do about this property. I will revisit you once I have done so. Now I must be on my way. I thank you for your time.'

The ride across the countryside to the second landholding took only an hour. Not that Sir Reginald noticed the time, he was lost in thought, deliberating on the awful news told to him by the priest. They arrived early afternoon at the four hundred acres which adjoined Clopton Hall, owned by William Clopton. Sir Reginald knew him, they hunted together on numerous occasions. He would be a good, and influential neighbour. The only community on the land was the hamlet of Alpheton.

As with the previous landholding, a large acreage was left for sheep to roam, eating the lush grass that covered the landscape year round. Here and there Sir Reginald saw fields of stubble left over from the harvesting of wheat, rye and barley (a staple for the production of ale). They would begin burning the stubble soon to clear for winter crops, or to leave fallow. In the distance they saw a shepherd herding a flock of sheep down the track towards Long Melford. They approached cautiously so as not to scare the animals. The shepherd had his crook, with a cow horn attached at one end. Both men watched with admiration as the shepherd put pebbles in the horn, launching them in front or to one side of the flock, gently guiding them in the direction he wanted. A skill borne of years of practice.

'Good morning. How goes your day my man?' asked Paul.

'It goes well sir. And who may you be? I do not recognize you from around these parts?'

'I am Paul, and this is my master, Sir Reginald Willoughby. He owns land to the west of here and is looking to rent this land from the Abbey. And your name?'

'I am known as Shepherd Peter, I live in Alpheton. So you may become our new landlords? I hope you will be fairer to your tenants than the Abbot and his thieves. Their greed knows no bounds.'

Sir Reginald raised his hands to stop the shepherd talking further, 'Hold your tongue man, such insolent talk will get you thrown in gaol—and worse, if said in front of the wrong people. However, you can trust me your thoughts will go no further. Tell me, I am interested to know what the Abbey does that causes you such angst?'

'Sire, it's what they don't do that causes us so much distress. They care not a jot for our wellbeing, or the upkeep of our houses. Just how many bales of wool we can produce, how many bushels of grain we grow to fill their coffers. For men of God they show little compassion.'

His mind still on the revelations from the priest at Rooksey Green, Sir Reginald felt a compulsion to see if this community's children were suffering similar depredations from the Abbey. He tried to think of a way to probe further without being too obvious. He approached the subject in a roundabout way, asking, 'Shepherd Peter, what is the number of people in your village?'
'I have heard it counted as high as 125, Sire. Why do you ask?'

'And of that, how many are young working men and women?'

Suddenly, the shepherd became evasive, 'That I couldn't say, Sire…though not as many as there should be.'

He looked away from the men, to his flock of sheep, quietly grazing on the grass verges. Deciding he had said enough, he excused himself, 'Sire, I'm afraid I cannot be more helpful on that score, you will need to talk to the priest there.'

Before Sir Reginald could ask another question, the shepherd pointed his crook down the track, saying, 'If you'll beg pardon sire, I need to get these sheep to market before evening. I wish you both a prosperous day.' With that, he clapped his hands and the flock moved forward, bleating in compliance.

Perplexed, Paul asked 'Sir, may I ask why you wanted to know how many children were living in the local village?'

'You may ask Paul but I won't answer, at least not yet. I have been informed of some potentially disturbing news which I must investigate further before I make it common knowledge. For your safety, it is best you know nothing of it.'

'As you wish sir. Now where to?'

With a sigh, Sir Reginald, looked around the undulating fertile Suffolk landscape. Despite everything he'd heard today, the opportunity to buy this land was too good to pass up. He would try and negotiate a better price with the Prior, if successful he would buy it. Overnight it would double his holdings and his wealth. As to the other matter he would have to think carefully about how to unearth the truths so as not to arouse suspicion, or accusations of heresy, from the Abbey.

'Paul, let us ride around the perimeter of the land then make our way back to the house, we have work to do, some property to buy,' declared Sir Reginald.

Transactions which would bring him a host of unwanted problems.

Chapter 8

~1535~

The Act of Supremacy of 28 November, 1534 formally made the English king head of the Church of England. Henry VIII now had no higher authority than God himself. In 1536, the King then made his first practical move in the long game of politics and religion that would become known as the English Reformation: Part of this move was to present Parliament with a bill to abolish all monasteries in his kingdom. It was called the Dissolution of the Monasteries.

The rain poured down, a drenching summer storm that only made the day even more depressing for the thousands who lined the streets to witness the funeral of Mary Tudor, Duchess of Suffolk. Also known as the French Queen, she was previously wedded to King Louis XII of France, and widowed after only three months of marriage. Mary subsequently returned to England to marry her true love, the Duke of Suffolk. She was also the sister of King Henry VIII and as befits a lady of such high rank, anyone who held a position of power or influence was at the Abbey to pay their last respects.

Unbeknown to any of the participants, this would be the last great Catholic celebration in the Abbey.

Henry VIII, unhappy that Rome would not allow him to divorce Katherine of Aragon, made the momentous decision to cut ties with the Catholic Church and found the Church of England, with him at its head.

Aside from the wide ranging constitutional and ecclesiastical changes it brought about, almost as important was the flow of money from the Catholic Church's vast estates, abbeys, and priories. All these and other sources of income from the Church would now swell the King's coffers. At this time, the Abbey of Bury St Edmunds was the fourth richest in the country. It would become a prime target for the King's *Valor Ecclesiasticus,* his new appointee to survey all the Catholic church's assets and what they were worth. (The sums are staggering, by one estimate it is about £2.5 billion in 2023 values.)

But for Sir Reginald Willoughby and his new wife Victoria, as they walk back from watching Mary Tudor's funeral, to their much improved house in Whyting street, they had other concerns to worry about.

They were both delighted with the news she was pregnant with their first child. The only sour note in their relationship has been the twelve-year-old son, Harold, from her previous marriage. To Sir Reginald's mind the boy was rude and ill behaved. Despite regular beatings, he had not shown him the deference and obedience he expected from a stepson. He needed further education on a how a young man should conduct himself, decided Sir Reginald.

Otherwise, he felt settled and content. It was now just over a year since he acquired the lands from the Abbey at the much reduced price of £110. It proved a quick and simple transaction, one devoid of much of the normal paperwork. The Prior claimed this kept the whole matter away from public scrutiny. The result made him one of the largest landholders in the area, and on paper, at least, very wealthy. He spent extravagant sums of money on the house to reflect his increased status—and to appease his new wife who only wanted the latest and the best for herself and their baby.

Whyting street itself was rapidly re-inventing itself as part of Bury, those with new wealth wished to live. No longer was Sir Reginald's the only large double winged house in the street. Several other merchants had built similarly impressive homes. Whyting street was becoming a showcase for Bury's *nouveau riche*. The street was wide, so even with two or three storey houses jutting out over the pavement there was plenty of light. The street was not yet paved, however a group of residents were planning to pool resources to change the earthen surface into something more durable. In the meantime, a crew of ragged urchins were paid pennies a day to keep it clear of manure, offal, and other foul smelling waste.

The accusations made against the Abbey concerning the disappearance of the village's children, Sir Reginald had done little about. Too busy with domestic matters and his business, they slipped from his mind. He had not returned to either village since he first surveyed them eighteen months ago.

The New Year saw the house with more modern conveniences, a "necessary" had been built outside, meaning the daily ritual of cleaning out chamber pots was no longer required. There were plans to dig out a cellar to create a cold store to provide a year round way of keeping meat and vegetables at a cool temperature, reducing waste and cost. Many other improvements were planned, the couple wanted the house to display their wealth in as many ways as possible.

The year 1536 dawned wet and cold. It had snowed for days, a rarity in East Anglia. Sir Reginald and Victoria huddled in the relative warmth of their grand home, anxiously awaiting the birth of their child. But of greater consequence to the country at large, was King Henry VIII's Act of Supremacy which recently came into effect, followed by another edict, The Act of Treason. Both cemented his position as the head of the new Church of England, severing nearly one thousand years of control by the Catholic Church in Rome. In simple terms, the population would soon be expected to renounce their Catholicism and become adherents to the new Church of England. A move that would result in decades of strife affecting practically every family in the realm.

But that was far from their mind as Victoria gave birth on March 16th to an, initially, healthy boy. They named him Henry. As the year progressed he fell for one illness after another. The sickly child managed to reach his first birthday, but was pale and weak. His parents paid physicians and apothecaries large sums of money to help cure his succession of ailments, nothing seemed to help. They prayed for the best, but feared the worst.

In April 1536, Sir Reginald visited one of his lenders in Brentgovel street, just off the Market Square. Barely had the meeting begun when he heard the Town Crier ringing his bell and bellowing for people's attention. They both left the meeting and walked outside to see what announcement was so important.

It was chilling news. King Henry VIII had brought into law the Act of Suppression, the first stage of what would become known as the Dissolution of the Monasteries. A way for Henry VIII to collect their income and boost his coffers. It was now illegal to send any money to the Church of Rome. The early stages were modest—the closure of all the smaller monasteries with an income of under £200. The sale of their assets would be handled by something called a Court of Augmentation.

After hearing this astounding news, the two men walked back to recommence their meeting. Sir Reginald was worried about how this change might affect him, but he also saw an opportunity to buy more land from the now defunct Catholic church. He sat down opposite Jeremiah Goldsmith, his long term lender and, as much as a banker can be, a friend.

'What do you make of these announcements Jeremiah? Maybe there is more land to be had at bargain prices?'

Jeremiah looked up from a roll of figures on his desk, shaking his head, 'Sir Reginald, looking at your account, you are fully mortgaged as far as I am concerned. Your income from the new landholdings is the only thing keeping you solvent. Rents from your other properties are insufficient to cover your repayments to me. I would not be willing to loan you any more money, no matter how tempting the lands being sold off might be. I would advise you to concentrate on making your existing assets as profitable as possible. Be warned I may also have to put up my interest rates if I suffer any more bad debts. I foresee difficult times ahead with all these monastic land sales. It could depress prices.'

Sir Reginald, unsettled by this blunt warning, replied, 'I know I owe you a considerable sum, but rest assured I will not default.'

'I have every faith you will continue to be a responsible borrower but I would counsel against making any further purchases, for I would not be able to help you. If there becomes a widespread sale of the Abbey's assets, I fear it could jeopardise the values of the properties you, indeed everyone, currently owns in the county.'

'Your point is well taken Jeremiah, I will certainly bear it in mind.' They exchanged a few more pleasantries before Sir Reginald bade his farewells and walked back through the town centre. Tomorrow was Saturday, market day when traders from miles around came to the town to sell their wares. There had been a market or Bury Fair since the early 1100s mainly selling corn, cheese and meat. Now there were many other vendors offering food, housewares and ready to eat meals. Further away in St Mary's Square were the horse and cattle markets.

Already some stall holders were setting up as he weaved his way amongst them, deep in thought at what he had heard from the town crier, and his pessimistic lender. He did stop to read the official notice pinned up for all to see. As few people could read, most relied on those that could to repeat the words of the Act of Suppression, or at least its most important points. One person was in the middle of reading the lengthy proclamation to an attentive audience. He could hear mutters of approval at the King's plans. Few had any sympathy for the Abbey and its incessant demands for money and tithes, while giving little back to the commoners.

Few realised its implications would shake the very foundations of their existence for years to come Affecting every person, every household, pauper or lord in ways they could not imagine. The first to feel its effects would be the Abbey, its Abbot, monks and nuns, then rippling out to the rest of the country. There were unsettling times ahead and Sir Reginald knew he had to think of ways to weather the coming storm.

A shock awaited him as he reached his house, outside was Father Richard Smith from Rooksey Green and a young waif of a girl standing by his side. Sir Reginald hesitated, now suddenly feeling guilty he had done nothing about the concerns raised by the priest when they first met, 'Father...it is good to see you again. What brings you here? And who is this young girl? Is there a problem you need to discuss? Please, do come inside.'

The priest nodded his thanks, guiding the girl before him as they entered the house. Sir Reginald indicated they should sit by the fire to warm themselves. He summoned one of the servants to bring food and wine, then asked that she go and find his wife, explaining they had some unexpected guests.

By the time the refreshments arrived, Victoria had come downstairs. She concealed her shock at seeing a bedraggled, elderly priest and a dirty, thin and painfully shy girl, busy gulping down some bread, cheese and mutton. Despite her ragged

94

clothes hanging limply on her, Victoria thought she saw a swelling belly indicating she was with child. Heavens she thought, this girl can only be fourteen or fifteen.

He had not told Victoria anything about the accusations made by the priest many months ago. So the conversation that followed caused her surprise and distress. It appeared the young girl, called Anna, had been abducted three years ago by those employed on behalf of the Abbey to find such youngsters. She was taken to the Abbey at Thetford, some ten miles north of Bury. There she had been sent out to work, when not being abused by the nuns and monks for their sexual pleasures.

Once she became pregnant they had no use for her. She was expelled to fend for herself. With the help of some caring farm workers, she made her way back home to Rooksey Green. However, for weeks the girl refused to say anything about her treatment, claiming the Abbey would evict her parents, and leave them destitute. Finally, she was persuaded to retell her tragic and sordid story to the priest. He believed that with this information something could now be done to bring these terrible atrocities out into the open. And the perpetrators brought to justice.

On hearing the details of the girl's abuses, Victoria turned angrily to her husband, 'Reginald, why did you not tell me about this before? We could have rescued this poor girl, and who knows how many others, months ago? We must go to the Abbey, talk to the Abbot. Maybe seek out Lord Rawlings, isn't he the Justice of the Peace? Surely he could do something, are you not an acquaintance of his? Please Reginald this cannot be allowed to continue.'

Sir Reginald, taken aback by the vehemence of his wife's criticism, tried to placate her. 'Of course my dear, let me consider our next course of action. We cannot rush into this, even with this poor girl's evidence...'

His condescending and evasive tone did not sit well with Victoria. Her eyes blazing with fury she spat back, 'Consider our next move? Reginald, you've had over a year to do something. All that time this girl and who knows how many others, have been suffering. If you won't do something immediately, I will!' On the verge of tears, she flounced out of the great hall, slamming the door behind her and ran up the stairs to her bedroom.

Later that day, after the priest and the girl departed, Sir Reginald sat next to his wife on the bed, trying to find some way of telling her that he could do little to help children like Anna.

'Victoria my love, even if what that girl and the priest are saying is true, the Abbot is the law in this town, and has jurisdiction over all the abbeys and churches in this part of the county. If we are to ask him to investigate this we need more proof, not the word of some pauper girl. Who will believe her? As for Lord Rawlings, I will talk to him, but I fear he will say the same. It is unfortunate, but with the power the church wields, this is an unwinnable battle at the moment. I am so sorry.'

Victoria reluctantly conceded the truth in her husband's words. 'I know, I know you're right, Reginald. But did you see that girl? She was only thirteen! And with child, how could men of God do this to someone so young? They will surely rot in hell.'

Taking his wife's comment as a way to finish the conversation, he agreed, 'You are right my dear, even if justice cannot be served on earth I pray these evil men and women will face God's and suffer accordingly.'

Chapter 9

~1537~

In England, the Catholic Church is no more. Its buildings, grand and modest, that once housed its devout adherents are being torn down and sold off. The monks, Abbots and nuns are generously offered pensions (in the case of St Edmundsbury's last Abbot, John Reeve of Melford, it is a staggeringly large amount, some £300 a year—when the average worker earned just £5. He is therefore comfortably cushioned from the blow of losing his prominent role in the town. Forty-two other monks are also pensioned off).

In 1537, Nicholas Bacon of Drinkstone became Solicitor to the newly appointed Court of Augmentations and enthusiastically started to dismantle and sell off the properties owned by the Abbey. Many are gifted to the King's favourites like the Dukes' of Norfolk and Suffolk. There is a frenzy of speculation, land being bought then resold at huge profits. Values go up and down by the week.

The following year, in September 1538, the King's Commissioners arrived at Bury Abbey to confiscate its remaining wealth. Their haul is a huge one, gold, silver and other valuables of almost incalculable value, making their way back into the King's coffers. The county's once powerful, wealthy centre of religious and legal power is no more.

Sir Reginald and Victoria have welcomed another child into this turbulent, uncertain world, a sturdy blonde boy called Benedict. He is bonny and healthy, in sharp contrast to his still sickly three-year-old brother, Henry who spends more time in his bed than crawling around their ever more luxurious house. Worryingly, he has great difficulty in seeing anything except the brightest of sunlight.

'Perhaps it is just as well Henry cannot walk, I fear he will injure himself by falling down the stairs. One wonders if his eyesight will ever improve?' Sir Reginald asked Victoria one evening over supper.

'I often wonder that too, it must be some kind of disease he is suffering from. I feel so helpless. I have been rubbing his eyes with a potion provided by our apothecary, it has made little difference except to make him cry in pain.'

Sir Reginald shook his head in sorrow, 'My poor Henry, it is a terrible affliction, blindness. I pray every day for it to heal, so far they have gone unanswered. I do fear for his future with such a disability.'

Henry never regained his sight, or lived to see his next birthday. One day, while playing near the River Lark, the maid took her eye off him for one moment. He fell in and drowned before she even noticed he was missing. The distraught parents now lavished their attention and wealth on their house and new son Benedict, who seems to have difficulty hearing their words, but he is young and they pray he will develop into a perfectly healthy young man.

New rugs now adorn the walls and floors. The whole home has been whitewashed giving it a clean and fresh aura. Sir Reginald, desperate to keep his depressed wife surrounded by only the best, has stretched his finances to the limit. It pains him to see so much monastic land being sold off, frequently at bargain prices, but he is unable to raise any more money to purchase these properties. The money lenders are making handsome profits from funding this land grab, but only to those they feel confident can repay it. Sir Reginald is not one of them.

He was working in his study late in October when a servant announced there was someone from the Court of Augmentations to see him. To arrive without an appointment was breaching etiquette, however Sir Reginald, wondering what this person wanted, one he has had no dealings with beforehand, agreed to see him.

A small man clutching a sheaf of papers, self importantly busy bodied his way into the study and sat down. He introduced himself as one of the Clerks to the Court of Augmentations, one Cecil Brownsmith. He wasted no time in getting to the point of the meeting. He brought news that put the fear of God into Sir Reginald.

Pulling out some rolls of paper he squinted at them, holding the words inches from his half closed eyes.

'…Let me see here, ah yes. You purchased two landholdings back in 1534, approximately 850 acres near Long Melford and Lavenham for the sum of…where is it, £110? Correct?'

Sir Reginald answered with a sinking feeling in his stomach, 'Yes that is correct. I can find the paperwork and deed if you wish, Mr Brownsmith? I have to ask. Is there a problem?'

'Yes there is I'm afraid Sir Reginald, it seems all is not in order. The sale was not authorised by the Abbot at the time, but was undertaken by one of the Priors without his knowledge. The man concerned acted in a fraudulent manner, and sold off several such parcels of land without the authority to do so. It therefore appears to the Court the land still belongs to the Abbey?'

'That cannot be so!' exclaimed Sir Angus angrily. 'I have all the paperwork, let me find it for you. It is proof I paid for the land in good faith.' It took a few minutes rummaging through an overflowing trunk of papers, before he found the purchase agreements and handed them to the sceptical clerk. He read them quickly.

'While I don't doubt sir, these appear to be genuine documents, they represent a fraudulent transaction. I see they were not notarised? I fear sir that if you wish to keep these lands you will have to pay for them again, legally.'

Sir Reginald was quivering with fury, 'Pay for them again? Why this is extortion sir! I bought that land in good faith for £110, it is mine and I intend to keep it.'

The Clerk was unfazed by his outburst, 'I understand your indignation, Sir Reginald, indeed you are one of many local businessmen duped by the Prior, but these papers are worthless. The court will not recognize their legitimacy. However, anticipating this might happen, the Court has authorised me to accept a payment of £150 to ensure ownership becomes legally yours. I can give you thirty days to facilitate this if you wish? Otherwise the lands will revert to the Court and be sold to the highest bidder.'

Sir Reginald was at a loss for words, but not visions that flashed through his mind of the humiliation and financial hardship he would suffer as a result of this misfortune. He'd been duped, and made to look a fool, that information could not become public. He merely nodded his acknowledgement of the Clerk's news, then watched numbly as he rose from the chair, wished him well, and walked out of Sir Reginald's study. He sat unmoving for almost an hour playing over in his mind the shattering news and how he could have been so careless, so gullible. He knew at the time something felt odd about the deal, but his greed for a bargain had pushed aside all reason and doubt. Now he was paying the price. His thoughts moved onto how he could exact revenge on, or get his money back from, the dishonest Prior. Presuming he could find him.

It took several weeks of discreet enquiries, and the cajoling of favours from those he knew close to the Court of Augmentations before Sir Reginald found out more about the man who embezzled his money. The ex-Prior, who now went by the name Christian Cooper had, wisely, fled the Abbey soon after the Court arrived. He left behind a trail of dishonest dealings affecting at least ten other local businessmen. Sir Reginald contacted some of them he knew and they agreed to start an investigation as to Cooper's whereabouts. The Court of Augmentations was happy for them to undertake the search only asking he be brought before them once found. More weeks followed as Sir Reginald and the other businessmen used their contacts to ascertain the ex-Prior's whereabouts. He was finally discovered living in some comfort, in Halstead, Essex.

Sir Reginald and a party of three other businessmen all of whom suffered at his dishonest hands, made the day-long trek to Halstead and found his large residence with ease. They confirmed with a local inn owner that the ex-Prior was at the address they'd been given. They broke in at dawn, on a cold, dark morning and unceremoniously roused him from his bed. Tied to a chair, his captors proceeded to vent their wrath on him. After a particularly painful beating, he confessed to his duplicitous dealings. Christian begged not be taken back to Bury St Edmunds and face justice, offering them the huge sum of £500 in gold to let him go. Deciding to play the crook at his own game, they agreed to his deal, took his money, then threw him into the cart for the journey back to the Assize Court in Bury.

He screamed his frustration at being duped, threatening them all with untimely ends once he was released.

They ignored his profane protestations. They gagged him and trundled northwards towards Sudbury, then onwards to Bury. However, it was to be Christian Cooper's unlucky day, twice over. As the group passed by the hamlet of Alpheton they came across villagers' working in the fields. As they stopped to allow the horses to rest, some of the farmworkers wandered over to see who the prisoner was in the back of the cart.

One man peered at Christian and jumped back in surprise. He turned to the others, 'Isn't that him? The man who came here for our children? Am I mistaken?' He called the others to the cart, 'Here, all of you! Do you recognize this piece of shit?'

They crowded round, poking him so he couldn't hide his face with his hands. 'That's him! The perverted bastard who's stolen our young 'uns. We should hang him here and now!'

Christian's eyes bulged with fear, he shook his head vigorously, silently denying the accusation though the gag. Sir Reginald rode up to the cart, pushing away the irate crowd, 'Men, please let us not have any rough justice here today. This man is going back to face the Court for fraud and stealing. If he is guilty of these other crimes, then let him be tried for those as well. He will go to gaol I am sure. He may be hanged. But we must let the proper process take its course.'

Trying to keep his optimism under control, Sir Reginald couldn't believe his good fortune. He had recovered his stolen money and then found the man responsible for the abhorrent crimes committed against these people's unfortunate children. He was secretly delighted, Victoria would feel likewise.

'He deserves worse than that, hang him, hang him!' The crowd took up the chant. This chance meeting was turning into a mini riot. Sir Reginald did not like the way the mood was changing. It could get nasty very quickly, particularly for their prisoner. There were not enough of them to take on Sir Reginald and his group, but it could turn bloody, something he wanted to avoid. Deep down he realised, a part of him would be quite

104

happy to see this odious man meet an untimely end. Worriedly, he looked at his group. There was almost a collective shrug of shoulders. They cared not. They had recouped nearly all their financial losses with his golden bribe. He was of no further use to them.

Feeling the need to obtain more evidence that the hapless Christian was indeed who the rabble claimed, he tried to placate them, 'We need more proof he is the person you say he is. I will send someone to Rooksey Green, the priest there has knowledge of this man. It will only take a short while to bring him here. If he agrees with you, then this man is all yours to do with as you see fit.'

Sir Reginald dispatched one of his party to find and bring back the priest. Within an hour, they returned. He walked over to him, 'Father Smith, thank you for coming. Please look at the man in the cart—do you recognise him?'

The Priest looked at the ex-Prior for a few seconds, then recognition dawned, 'By the Almighty, that is the man who came seeking our young children. Has he confessed to his dreadful crimes?'

'Not yet,' shouted one of the farm workers, 'But he soon will.' He turned to the crowd behind him, 'C'mon, let's give him some of his own medicine.' They grabbed the petrified man and dragged him out of the cart onto the ground. A free for all of kickings and beatings followed until Sir Reginald rode his horse so it was astride his bleeding body, preventing the mob from meting out their brand of justice.

'Wait! Stop this men! Let him talk, let us see what he has to say in defence!'

The gag was wrenched roughly off his face. Through a bloodied lip and broken nose, Christian blubbered a desperate plea for mercy, 'Please, I beg you, I was only doing the Abbey's wishes. I tried to stop them but they threatened to excommunicate me. Remember, you took money from us for your children, so you are not without guilt! You sold them to us!'

Father Smith couldn't control himself, he pushed Christian back to the ground and put his foot on his chest, 'My parishioners had no choice. Money or not, you were going to take them. You did that in an effort to salve your conscience. You are despicable and a shame on all men of the cloth. I hope you rot in a goal, then in Hell.'

One of the farmers pushed the priest aside, 'This evil fucker won't see no gaol, but he'll see Hell soon enough…c'mon boys let's hang him now. He doesn't deserve the chance to flee again.'

A length of rope was pulled from the back of the cart and a noose thrown around Christian's neck. He was stripped naked, then still screaming and begging for mercy dragged across the road to an old oak tree. Within minutes, he was dangling by his neck, eyes bulging, feet kicking maniacally in his death throes. One man, pitchfork in hand, walked up to his still alive, swinging body. In a swift, vicious, movement he launched the pitch fork handle burying it deep between the man's buttocks.

'And that's for my daughter you piece of scum. May you rot in hell.'

Chapter 10

~1537~

Victoria, was incensed, 'You let them murder that man? Why did you not bring him to Bury to face justice?'

Sir Reginald tried to remain composed in the face of his wife's anger, 'He received the justice he deserved Victoria, and there was little we could do in the face of such an irate mob.' He hated lying, but it was the best excuse he could come up with on the spur of the moment. 'There were just too many of them. It was all over very quickly, at times we feared for our lives so violent had the villagers become towards us and the former Prior.'

Victoria, exasperated, replied, 'I care not for his death. Think, Reginald; if you had brought him back to the gaol, the guards could have made him reveal who his accomplices were. Then the whole network of perverts could have been brought to justice. Now we know nothing of them, or where they might be?'

His wife made an excellent point, he had to admit. Hells bells, he kicked himself. An opportunity to bring all those child kidnappers and abusers to book had been lost in a moment, of, let's be honest, he told himself, the satisfaction of seeing that slime bucket beg for his life and hang.

His wife stopped haranguing him and now demanded, 'I think you owe it to all the poor girls and boys, and their parents in the villages on your lands to seek out the other perpetrators and bring them before the courts. It is the least you can do. You would do so if it was our children who had similarly suffered. As a man of honour, I'm sure you'll agree.'

He didn't agree, at all. But he knew better than to ignore Victoria, and knew she was right. He just didn't see himself galloping around the countryside finding the victims, then seeking out their abusers. However, if he didn't do something, he would forever feel guilty, and Victoria would never allow him to forget it. He brought the discussion to a close with a promise he would do as she suggested.

Over the next few months, Sir Reginald, with help from the Justice of the Peace paid for, and organised, a group of trustworthy men to visit all the villages on Sir Reginald's landholdings and report on the number of children that had been taken, and if possible talk to any that may have returned. Thereby gathering as much information as possible as to where they had been held and the names of any of their abusers.

In September 1537, Sir Reginald met with his group of investigators and the Sheriff of Norfolk and Suffolk, Sir William Drury. They were both aware of a salacious report called the

Comperta Monastica recently compiled by supporters of King Henry, which detailed (many claimed untruthfully) sordid details of sexual misconduct among the inhabitants of holy places around the country—and Suffolk was no exception.

His long standing assistant, Paul Huntingdon, had been in charge of the group of investigators. They visited villages not just on Sir Reginald's land, but many others across Suffolk.

Nervously, he stood up to present their findings. It made for distressing and horrifying listening. 'My Lords, over the last six months we have visited twenty-five villages across the county of Suffolk. In sixteen cases, we discovered claims of children, boys and girls forcibly taken from their homes by people saying they represented the Church or some form of local authority. Most said the children were needed to help run and work in various holy places. They were promised the children would receive an education, decent living conditions and be free to leave after five years. That this was being done with the blessing of the highest authorities in the county.

'My Lords, these are poor, ill educated, illiterate peasants who had no reason to doubt these men, and even if they did, could do little to protest or stop these abductions. We estimate as best we can tell, that some seventy-eight children over the last five years have been so abominably treated.'

The room sat quiet as this sickening news was digested. Sir William Drury asked, 'Did you find any children that returned from these abductions? If so, could they shed light on what happened to them—and where?'

'Very few, my Lord,' replied Paul. 'Just a handful came forward to admit they escaped their captors. All confirmed what we already knew. They were treated badly, abused by members of both sexes, received no education and were treated, it seems, as slaves. Furthermore, if the girls became pregnant with child, they were sent to workhouses far away. The boys fared little better. If they became ill, they too were sent away, no one is certain where. However, the only monastic houses where these activities took place were at Sudbury, Clare and Ixworth.'

For another hour, Sir Reginald and Sir Robert peppered Paul and his group with questions, trying to gauge the extent of this dreadful traffic in young people in their county. If that number had been abducted from twenty five villages—how many across the whole county? It didn't bear thinking about.

'There are over forty monasteries, abbeys and convents in Suffolk,' explained Sir Robert. 'And our task is not helped as several of the smaller ones are already dismantled, the effects of the King's Dissolution Act are taking effect very quickly. It means most of the likely perpetrators have left. Tracking them down will be difficult to say the least, I'm afraid the money and resources are not available to launch any such inquiry Sir Reginald. Indeed as these places are closed down, we will undoubtedly see the end of this pernicious activity. I sincerely hope so.'

Sir Robert stood up and left the room, leaving Sir Reginald wondering what he could do next without the support of the sheriff. The end was not satisfactory, but it was a conclusion that over the next few years saw some of the children reunited with their parents as the monastic houses were closed. Many never returned.

As the inhabitants of the holy houses were evicted many sought refuge in local villages and towns. Inevitably from time to time, they came face to face with their captives. Those that did received swift vigilante justice inflicted upon them by those that had suffered such terrible injuries at their hands.

In 1540, such an unreported incident occurred concerning John Cotton, the former Prior of Sudbury Priory. Evicted when the building was given to Thomas Eden, he retired to a small house in the nearby village of Stoke by Clare. John was aware that some of the children abducted and once "working" in the Priory now had returned to their villages. However, he felt safe that his reputation would provide protection from any accusations laid against him. After several months living in rural seclusion, on a small but comfortable pension, he felt safe enough to venture into Sudbury on market day.

There, by a divine coincidence some would later claim, one of the young girls, Bonnie, that suffered at his, and the other monk's hands, saw him. She was working on her father's vegetable stall when he came to buy some onions. For a second, Bonnie froze in terror at seeing her tormentor again. She could still remember the look of pleasure on his sweating face as he beat and raped her, while other monks held her down and then took their turn abusing and defiling her.

She managed to control her shock long enough to serve him. As she handed him the vegetables the former Prior smiled and said thank you, no recognition showing on his face. Ashen and shaking, she walked over to her father. Bonnie quickly explained what happened and pointed out John Cotton as he stood at a nearby stall inspecting some fruit.

111

'Are you sure it was him?' Her father, Jonathan asked, holding her at arm's length looking into her tear filled eyes. She nodded. With no further words spoken, Jonathan calmly walked over to his sons and whispered instructions to them. They both left the stall and discreetly followed their sister's attacker.

It was early evening when the former Prior left Sudbury on his old mule for the five mile journey back to his cottage in Stoke by Clare. As he passed through the woods near Borley, Jonathan and his two sons were waiting. They launched themselves from the undergrowth taking their victim by total surprise, dragging him off the mule and into the woods far from the track.

His body was never found. If it had been, the sight would have turned even the hardiest of stomachs. After extracting the names of other members of the Priory who, their terrified captive claimed, were the real culprits in the mistreatment of young children, John Cotton had his genitals cut off and while still alive forced into his mouth. They did little to stifle his screams of agony, as the three men took out their anger and hatred on his naked body, prolonging his misery for over an hour. Finally, when Jonathan's axe severed the last of John Cotton's limbs from his body, the mutilated former Prior went to meet his fate in the afterlife.

The three men quickly dug a shallow grave, and left the scene of their crime satisfied justice had prevailed. Jonathan now had six other names that needed the same penalty dispensed upon them. They intended to show them the same mercy they had for John Cotton.

Chapter 11

~1550s~

Harold, the sixteen-year-old son of Sir Reginald and Victoria was somewhere specifically forbidden by his parents—the ruins of the Abbey. He continued to be a thorn in his father's side, but he cared not. There was too much fun to be had scrambling around the vast Abbey's crumbling buildings.

In the years since the Dissolution, it was first ransacked of its riches by the King and thereafter, by the population of the town. The inhabitants systematically dismembered the buildings, helping themselves to vast quantities of materials, carrying them off to build and repair their own houses. Cartfuls were pillaged, unchallenged by any authority. Years later, all that remained was a dangerous labyrinth of crumbling walls, collapsed roofs, broken glass and debris spread over acres of the once sacred Abbey grounds.

Also missing are the sacred remains of St Edmund. The main reason for centuries believers by the thousands made the pilgrimage to Bury and contributed to the town's immense wealth and prestige. Since the Dissolution, they were hidden, but no one knew where, or by whom. Locals believed it was either some well meaning monk or nun who saved the relics, fearing the King or his henchman would destroy them. Or, more likely, the new owner of the lands upon which the Abbey stood, John Eyer, disposed of them at the request of the Receiver General of Suffolk, a close friend of the King. They were, literally, a relic the King wanted destroyed.

Many years later, this scene of destruction was still being picked over, though anything usable or valuable had long since gone. Now the grounds and stubs of buildings became a treacherous playground for the towns' youngsters. The closure of the Abbey also meant the closing of all schools. Until new sponsors and money were found, the town's youth were enjoying their freedom, frequently amusing themselves amongst the Abbey's ruins.

Harold and his friend Helen were exploring what once was the Cloisters, a large square where the monks and nuns would walk and meditate. The recent collapse of a roof and supporting panelled wall had exposed what appeared to be a door leading to…where? Harold was looking for excitement not treasures and this looked promising. He tentatively prodded at the door with his foot. It didn't move. He pulled away some rubble and fallen masonry to access it more easily.

He put his shoulder to it and pushed. Nothing gave, he shouted across the cloisters to Helen, 'Hey come and look at this old door, it was part of some panelling. Help me open it, let's see if it leads anywhere interesting.'

Helen, ever the sensible one, hesitated, she didn't really share his enthusiasm for this peculiarly male activity of scrabbling around in the dirt to find treasure, fun, or whatever they perceive to be a way to waste time. Nevertheless, she joined him and looked disinterestedly at the broken panels and the dark hole behind them. She tried to dissuade him from investigating further.

'Harry, your mother and father will punish you—and me—if you come to any harm. Be careful this wall looks very unstable. I think we should leave before you injure yourself, she grabbed his hand and tried to pull him away from the door.

However, Harold was a tall, strong boy, he easily freed himself from her grasp. This secret door had piqued his interest, he wouldn't take no for an answer. Impatient at her unwillingness to take any risks, Harold ignored her warnings and tested the panelling with a sound push with his ample shoulder. It moved a few inches. 'Come on, help me here Helen, don't be a dullard. Give me a hand here, I promise I won't do anything unwise.'

'A little late for that I think,' grumbled Helen. Reluctantly, she joined him and together they gave the solid oak panel a concerted push. It moved enough for them to see what was on the other side. The light from the open door revealed a space the size of a large cupboard, big enough for one, maybe two men.

Initially disappointed, Harold poked his head inside and looked at the floor. He got down on his knees and peered at the wooden boards, puzzled; he shouted back over his shoulder, 'Helen, looks like there's some kind of handle attached to a trap door in the ground. I'll see if I can pull it up.' He prised the handle loose and tugged on it, to his surprise it opened and a waft of cool air brushed his long hair. He couldn't see down further than a few feet, enough, though, to ascertain there were steps roughly carved out of the chalk foundation—the rock that the whole of the town was built upon.

His voice rose in excitement, he stood up, brushed himself down and told Helen, 'There's a passage of some description down there. I wonder where it leads? I've heard tales that when the Abbey was first built, the monks and nuns had tunnels excavated all under the town as stores and ways to escape attackers. Do you think this could be one of them?'

Helen had seen and heard enough, 'Harry I neither know, nor care. All I do know is if we are not back to our homes for supper, then a beating awaits us both. Let's come back in a day or two for a closer look?' Of course, Helen had no intention of returning, she hoped her vague promise of a future visit would soon be forgotten by the impetuous young man. The thought of descending into some centuries old tunnel was not her idea of fun.

She tugged again at Harry's arm, and this time leant and pecked him on the cheek, whispering in his ear, 'Come on Harry, I have a better way to spend a few minutes before we go home…" He smiled in anticipation. The promise of some kissing and fumbling of Helen's firm young breasts, suddenly filled him with an urge more compelling than an underground tunnel.

The delights of his discovery in the Abbey were soon forgotten as he groped inexpertly under her clothing. She might be only sixteen but was generously endowed and already familiar with the power and control a woman's body could have over a man's thoughts and actions. It was too soon for Harold to

116

take her virginity, that he would only have once in the marital bed. For a few minutes, she let him ineptly rub her breasts and tease her nipples. He wasn't a great kisser either. However, she knew his technique in the foreplay department would improve under her tutelage, he was a keen and eager pupil.

Helen had him hooked, he was smitten with her-and her young body. Now it was a question of gradually reeling him in until he was caught in her net. He was a desirable catch. A tall, strongly built handsome boy, with blonde hair full of curls, blue eyes and a wispy fair beard. More importantly, the makings of a good career as an accountant for his father. His family lived in a substantial house on Whyting street—a favourable part of the town, and owned significant landholdings spread around Suffolk. Occasionally Helen admitted to herself, she was becoming fond of this impetuous, adventurous young man. Maybe next time they were alone, she might allow him to explore her body a little further. Keep him interested without getting too carried away. A delicate balance, though one she felt confident she could maintain long enough to land him into marriage.

After three days, Harold's curiosity overpowered him. With Frederick, his next door neighbour, he returned to the scene of his discovery in the Abbey. Frederick was only fifteen, a small, nervous boy, suffering from poor sight due to a childhood illness of some kind. He therefore, was not an ideal companion for an adventure into the depths of an underground tunnel, but at least he would do as asked by Harold, unlike Helen who continually demanded he be *careful* and *sensible*.

Harold brought along candles and a tinder box with which to light them. The boys pulled back the wooden panelling that Harold and Helen had discovered at the entrance to the tunnel.

117

With a candle each they descended into the pitch black passage. The steps down were roughly hewn and slippery with damp. They counted twenty before they reached the bottom. Ahead they could see nothing, the candles lit up only a few feet in front of them. The tunnel's roof grazed Harold's head, making him occasionally duck to avoid painfully banging it on the unforgiving rock. If he stretched his arms out, he could easily touch the walls. A frisson of excitement and trepidation made him shiver. He wondered: Why had this been built? Who were the last people to use it? What might be hidden down here?

They walked a few yards, the darkness was all encompassing, almost tangible beyond the dim arc of their candlelight, enveloping them like a black cloak. To Frederick, the little cocoon of light thrown by the candles was scary and claustrophobic.

Frederick began to whine, 'I think we should go back Harold, I am not comfortable down here. Let us return to the surface before we injure ourselves.'

'No one is going to get hurt Frederick, it's just a tunnel...afraid some ghosts may be here? Or some other demons waiting to attack you?' Harold teased.

'Jest not Harold, these could be crypts, full of dead bodies, I know not what might be here, and I do not wish to find out. I will wait for you at the top of the stairs. Unless you are coming with me?'

'If you wish to go back, do so, I am searching further. There may be something of interest down here, if so, I intend to find it.'

Panicky and chastised, Frederick disappeared back towards the steps.

Now Harold had only the light of one candle to illuminate his path. The ground beneath his feet was uneven with flint and other rocks protruding, making progress slow. He estimated he'd travelled, maybe one hundred yards when the tunnel split into two. He began to feel a little frustrated, so far he had discovered nothing. Surely there must be something of interest down here, why were these tunnels built if not to hide something or for storage?

In fact, he was unlikely to find anything of value. The tunnels were dug when the first Abbey was re-constructed in 1327 after the people of Bury had destroyed it in an act of rebellion against the authoritarian power of the Abbot. Fearful that such an event might re-occur, these series of escape tunnels were excavated spreading from the Abbey under Angel Hill all the way to houses in the old grid. There, carefully concealed exits to the surface were afforded via cellars and trapdoors.

Over the years rumours about such a network of escape tunnels had persisted among the townsfolk. Some claimed after a fall of snow the warmer air from the tunnels seeped up through the ground leaving melted tracks across the Angel Hill. Occasionally houses subsided into large holes which were said to be caused by the tunnels' roofs collapsing. Scaremongers suggested such tunnels were used to bury the dead from previous plagues—almost guaranteed to dissuade anyone from wishing to investigate them further.

Harold took the right hand tunnel. He noticed the incline was steepening—indicating he was still moving away from the river, towards the centre of the town. He stumbled on, the air becoming foetid and stale. Disheartened at finding not a single item of interest he turned around and started back towards the entrance. Suddenly, he felt something scurry across his feet. He instinctively jumped, painfully hitting his head on the tunnel roof. In the half light thrown by the candle he saw an enormous rat disappear into the impenetrable blackness. Rubbing his head to ease the pain he knew it must have come into the tunnels from another entrance than the one Harold had used. But where? He turned back, with a renewed sense of purpose and a burgeoning headache, walking as quickly as he could in the direction the rat disappeared, keen to find where it had come from.

After a few minutes, with the air now uncomfortable to breathe, and his head throbbing, Harold was on the verge of admitting defeat when saw an old wooden trap door in the tunnel roof.

Excited, he pushed against it, however it stuck fast, not moving an inch. He banged it with his fist in the vain hope someone might hear him. There was no reaction, just a dull echo within the tunnel. He was now feeling dizzy and a little faint, blood oozing down his face and neck. The cut on his head was worse than he thought. He sat down on the damp floor. Panic rose in his chest, if he passed out here, no one would find him. He felt his hand burning, the candle nearly used, the heat from the flame only an inch or two from his fingers. Soon it would expire..

He couldn't sit and do nothing. Quelling his rising anxiety, Harold stood up and walked quickly downhill towards the exit. He estimated it was a ten or fifteen minute walk. With a splutter, the candle died, the blackness became absolute. A feeling of terror took over. Was he going to die in this dark, damp hell hole!? He started to run, knowing he just had to follow the tunnel downhill to reach the steps up to fresh air and safety. Harold stretched his arms out to feel the side of the tunnel, guiding him down its centre. Suddenly his fingers sensed something different to the touch than cold, damp chalk. A smooth slab of stone. He stopped and in the pitch black, ran his fingers over its surface. There were some indentations…he could not see what they were but moving his fingers back and forth…they seemed to form letters of some sort.

Cursing he had no way to see, let alone copy the inscription, he tried to translate in his mind the shapes his fingers were sensing, into letters. He desperately wanted to remain playing this parlour game of imaginary letters and words and memorise as much as he could. But his headache and the stale air was making him feel ill. He committed to memory the first few letters, then left, now in a hurry to breath fresh air and transcribe what was in his mind before he forgot. He rushed down the tunnel slope, stumbled twice cutting his knees and hands, he felt nothing, the primal urge to survive dowsing any pain.

There, at last! A smudge of light in the distance, and the steps to escape this horror. He reached them, clambered up, breathless, heart palpitating, to see Frederick staring at him, a look of relief on his face. Harold collapsed onto the ground gasping in fresh air. After a few minutes, with help from Frederick he sat up, and gathered his wits. He needed to write down the letters quickly. Picking up a piece of broken panelling and a shard of flint, with a bemused Frederick looking on, he scratched the letters:

Reliquiae sancti h...
Ab...
Tutus ab..
Requi...

Frantically, Harold closed his eyes trying to recreate in his mind all the letters his fingers had traced just a few minutes earlier. His pulsating head made concentration impossible, not helped by Frederick's wittering questions. Frustrated, he gave up.

'Jesus, Harold, what's that mean? Are you delusional? You were gone a long time. I was getting really worried about you. Did you find anything? Are you badly hurt, your head looks in a sorry way. I think we must get home and clean the wound.'

Harold, waved dismissively at his concerns, 'Please Frederick desist with the inquisition! I shall be fine, thank you. It's just a scratch.'

Frederick had to ask, 'What are these letters you have just carved?'

'Yes I did, the biggest fucking rat you ever saw, size of a cat! And an inscription on a stone that started with these letters. Otherwise, nothing.' He held out his hand, 'Please, give me a pull up so we can make our way home. I fear my parents will be less than impressed with my exploits, and bloody injuries. It may be a while before I see you again!'

They made their way from the Abbey ruins up Churchgate street and into Whyting street. Harold by now was feeling lightheaded, leaning on the diminutive Frederick for support. By the time they reached his home, Harold was close to collapse. Frederick guided him indoors to a seat in the great hall. He asked a passing servant for a bowl of water and some cloth to wash his friend's wounds. Before he could administer any assistance, Victoria walked in, saw the blood all over her son's head and neck and ran over to help. She asked the inevitable question.

'Please God my son, what have you done to yourself?' Before he could answer, Harold saw Frederick hastily excusing himself, as he wisely ran out of the house. He didn't wish to hear the tongue lashing he was about to receive. And he was right. Once his mother ascertained the wound looked worse than it was, she demanded to know how it happened.

Harold feebly pled his case, knowing nothing he could say would silence his Mother's anger, 'We were just exploring the Abbey ruins and I banged my head mother, nothing serious. Please don't be alarmed.'

'Harold I'm not alarmed, I'm angry that you went there despite your Father saying you shouldn't. You have deliberately disobeyed him. He will be annoyed and, I suspect, disappointed, in your behaviour. Those ruins are dangerous, as you have now painfully discovered. Once I have cleaned the wound I suggest you go to your bedroom and await your fate for when he returns.'

Harold didn't argue, there was no point. His mother wiped the blood off his head and found a bandage to dress it. He retired to his room hoping the throbbing in his head would subside

123

before he faced his father's wrath. As he lay down, he put his hand in his coat pocket and pulled out the piece of wood with the letters he'd hastily inscribed upon it. He tried to make sense of them:

Reliquiae sancti h…
Ab…
Tutus ab..
Requi…

Clearly it was Latin, a language he was familiar with from lessons at school. It was still widely used in history, philosophy and theology. But the brief amount he remembered yielded little sense when,

Reliquiae sancti, translated to: 'the relics of…'
Tutus ab, meant 'safe from'

The rest of the letters provided no clues. He put the piece of wood into a trunk at the end of his bed, lay down and went to sleep. He was awoken by his father shaking him awake to then promptly, and at some length, berate him for his stupidity and disobedience. As punishment, he was forbidden to see any of his friends for a week. It could be worse, thought Harold, there was no beating, his self inflicted injury causing him enough pain, no doubt his father reasoned. For the moment, all he wanted was the pounding in his head to stop.

Later that day, after slowly rising from his bed, he looked at the transcription. He had no idea if it described something important or not. Harold decided to hide it under a floorboard to re-examine some time in the future.

Like all teenage boys, his mind was easily diverted onto more exciting pastimes. His attention drawn towards the ever more accommodating Helen, and after several month's hiatus, the resumption of school. The enigmatic inscription gathered dust out of sight and mind and the piece of wood was left untouched, then forgotten. The Abbey ruins continued to be plundered for any remaining items of value. The secret door to the tunnel was crushed as the wall around it collapsed, and rubble filled the hole, sealing it shut.

It would be another 250 years before the tunnel was re-discovered and the inscription on the wall translated.

Chapter 12

~1578~

The Royal Progresses were an opportunity for both the people of Elizabethan England and the Queen herself to offer a glimpse into each other's world. They allowed the Monarch to assert her authority as she travelled around the country. It was also a huge logistical exercise with basically Elizabeth I taking her whole government "on the road" with her. This could mean up to a thousand people and all their accompanying luggage and possessions accompanied them. At each stop the hosts—normally a wealthy aristocrat—was expected to find accommodation and provide food for everyone on the Progress.

Elizabeth I embarked upon twenty-three of these highly choreographed and expensive endeavours during her forty-four-year reign.

'They are coming in through the Westgate, there's hundreds of them!'

Harold's two grandchildren came rushing into the great hall, excited that at last Elizabeth Ist's Progress across East Anglia had reached Bury. It was nearly one hundred years since a monarch visited the town, the last being in 1486. Harold grabbed his walking stick, made his way down the hall out into Whyting street.

They had moved into the house after his mother and father had died in an accident and left it to him in their Will. Their children were born while they were living in Fornham all Saints. They moved into the Whyting street house ten years ago.

How Helen would have loved to have seen this spectacle! But she died eight years ago, after almost twenty-five years of marriage, he still missed her warmth, humour and sound advice. One that had seen her give him five children, of whom only two survived; Michael and Gwendoline. It was Michael's two teenage grandchildren, Grace and Robert who had waited by the town walls for the first sight of the Queen's much anticipated arrival. They now came in with the news she was in Bury. They were staying with him just for this momentous occasion, leaving their parents at home in Rattlesden. He was enjoying their company, even if at times, it proved tiring, and worrying.

It was Michael who informed his grandfather about the Queen's imminent appearance. Grace, a tall raven haired beauty, with sparkling green eyes, fair skin and a permanent smile on her face, was unable to speak. She had been struck mute during an illness at Harold's house when three years old. Now a striking fourteen-year-old, she overcame her disability and communicated using her hands, facial expressions and writing on a slate, using words pared down to their bare minimum. She was beguilingly naive, seemingly unaware that her sparkling character and innocent looks made her dangerously attractive to men. Harold constantly worried that someone would take advantage, knowing she was unable to easily dissuade their advances or summon any assistance.

It took them twenty minutes to reach the Market Square, by which time the spearhead of the Queen's enormous entourage, containing over one thousand members of her court and government, were making their way down to the Abbey Palace where Sir Thomas Badby was to host Her Majesty for a four day stay. The Progress numbered so many, it stretched for over ten miles. It would be several hours before they all arrived. Anyone owning a large property with spare accommodation was asked to accommodate some of the entourage. The town's population would be increased by almost a third once everyone arrived. Harold would soon find out which members of the Progress intended to lodge at his house. Indeed so many were staying, some of the more senior members like Lord Burghley and Lord Leicester were residing some distance from the town.

By the evening, four men were making themselves at home in Harold's guest rooms in the north wing and two women took over one of the servant's rooms in the south wing. They were lowly members of the Progress: two clerks, two messengers and two seamstresses. For the first two days, they came and went to the Abbey Palace, leaving early, returning in the evening. They joined the family for dinner and regaled their hosts with the behind the scenes gossip, people, and the stories of life in the Royal Progress. Grace, in particularly, was mesmerised by what she heard.

On the evening of the second day, she knocked on the door of Harold's office. She was smiling, her eyes flashing with excitement, 'What is it Grace? You look very pleased with yourself!'

She walked over to his desk, took a piece of scrap paper and dipped the quill in the inkwell, writing hurriedly: *'inv to abbey tomorr, I go? pleas?'*

Harold tried to suppress a frown, he sought clarification, 'You've been invited tomorrow to the Abbey Palace? By whom?'

'Yes. guest toby,' her eyes were pleading with him. She nodded her head as if encouraging him to agree.

'Oh, Toby is one of the messengers staying here? What does he want to show you?' Harold felt the need to find out a little more, aware each answer was tortuously long winded.

Grace hastily scribbled, *'Downstairs. meet people. fun. be bk by supp. prom. Pleas!!!'* He was concerned, she was so young and innocent. He noticed her a couple of times scribbling notes to this young man over the dinner table. It seemed harmless enough. He was a rough type, though quite well spoken. Harold weighed up his decision. She had to be allowed a little freedom, the chance to meet people from outside of the town. After all, the young man was staying in his house, what harm could come of it?

He looked up, her imploring look melting any last resistance, 'Very well Grace, you may go. But I expect you back for supper tomorrow. Don't be late.'

She leant over and kissed him on the forehead then skipped out of the room, joyous and excited.

Toby had been a messenger in Queen Elizabeth's household for only a year. The son of a knight, he'd secured his position through friends of his father. He was a short, burly lad, long curly black hair framed a pox-scarred face. Toby couldn't be called handsome, but he exuded a rough charm Grace found attractive. He spoke with a coarse London accent and was full of stories about where he'd been as part of the Royal Progresses, the Earls and Dukes he'd met, the amazing castles and homes he'd stayed in. Grace was entranced with the tales he told. A life so far removed from hers. When he'd suggested they go behind the closed doors at the Abbey Palace so she could see for herself what it was like to be part of a Royal Progress, she couldn't contain her enthusiasm. Persuading her grandfather had been easier than she'd expected, then again, he was a soft touch when it came to her charms, and she knew how to deploy them to successful effect.

The Abbey Palace was a grand sight, though slightly ramshackled, made up of several buildings aside from the Palace itself. There was the King's Hall, a Tower, plus numerous outbuildings, stables and servants' quarters.

Remnants of the original Abbey could still be seen, parts of its ancient walls incorporated into newer structures. Toby took Grace's arm and led her around to the kitchen and servants' entrances. She stood captivated as a continuous flow of people rushed in and out of the Palace running errands, fetching supplies. It was organised chaos.

'Come follow me,' Toby tugged at her arm, 'Want to show you something special.' He led her down some worn stone steps into a cellar.

Momentarily, Grace held back, this did not seem a good idea. She shook her head.

'Honestly girl, it's nothing to be scared of, we'll only be down here a minute. There's lots of interesting stuff to see.' Grace relented and held his hand as they descended into the gloom. The cellar had a few candles throwing a dim light that didn't reach the farthest corners of the vast storage room. Grace wondered why she was here, what was so interesting? Suddenly out of the shadows two other young men appeared.

Toby with a smirk of achievement, announced, 'Here's the girl I was tellin' you about. Can't talk, so she can't shout or scream. Perfect for a bit of fun eh?'

The two men approached Grace as Toby held her arms so tightly she couldn't move. One felt her breasts the other grabbed between her legs. Grace, now petrified, shook her head, pleading soundlessly, pointlessly, for them to stop. Could this really be happening? If only she could shout for help, there were people just a few feet away up the stairs. Instead, all she could do was silently thrash around trying to break free of Toby's harsh grip. Meanwhile, the two others pawed and groped her. Laughing and making crude remarks as they forced their hands inside her bodice, the other lifted up her dress.

They dragged her further away from the steps into the semi-darkness. She could barely see their faces though through her tears she saw, one was bald, and the other had flowing blonde hair and a beard. They roughly pushed her to the ground, and tore at her clothing. She managed to bite one of their arms as he held her down, only to receive a thumping blow to her head rendering her stunned and limp with shock. Her legs were forced apart. She gasped in pain as Toby took her. A few moments later he grunted, stopped and got up, only to be replaced by one of the other young men. For what seemed like a day in hell she was abused and subjected to unspeakable degradations. Finally, laughing and congratulating Toby for finding "such a willing girl," the three boys left Grace lying on the ground, crying, stunned and bleeding.

Grace lay immobile with shock on the cold, damp cellar floor. She eventually recovered enough to stand up and walk. She staggered painfully to the top of the steps. Through her hysteria and pain she looked around at the rushing crowds of people, not sure what to do next. Grace tried to attract somebody's attention. She couldn't shout for help, for a moment, frustratingly, no one noticed her. Then suddenly her legs felt weak and she collapsed onto the ground, immediately attracting the attention of several servants. They gently picked her up and took her inside. Dazed, she sat by the fire, someone gave her a warm drink. Three girls hovered over her asking if she knew who attacked her? It took a while before they understood she couldn't talk. Though she needed to say nothing for them to understand the horrors she'd been subjected to. The blood on her face and down her skirt told a graphic story that needed no words. Once Grace had calmed down a little and felt able to walk, one of the girls offered to take her home.

Michael, Grace's father, her mother, Annette, brother Robert and Harold stood around Grace's bed looking down at the poor girl's bruised face. She was finally asleep after the physician had dispensed some laudanum.

'We are sure it was this boy Toby that did this?' asked Michael, his face was taut with anguish, his voice struggling not to crack with emotion. He looked down at his beautiful, defenceless daughter, the rage boiling inside him. How could anyone do such a thing to an innocent girl? Never before had he felt the urge to kill someone. He knew if he caught her abusers he would take their lives without a qualm of conscience. They deserved to die for inflicting this pain on his beloved daughter.

'That's what she wrote on her tablet before she fell asleep. He was our guest here,' Harold replied in a whisper. He continued in a voice full of remorse, 'I must take responsibility for putting Grace in the way of such danger. I should have never allowed her to go there. That boy must be punished. I am seeing Sir Thomas Badby this evening. I expect him to make every effort to catch her rapists. This is a heinous crime committed on his property—he must act, and quickly, before the Queen's Progress travels to Norwich.'

They had obtained little other information from an almost catatonic Grace, just it was Toby and two other men who had raped her. The gloom of the cellar had made it difficult to see their faces in detail. Not wishing to upset her they did not ask more questions for fear of distressing her further. With that meagre knowledge they made their way to the Abbey Palace.

It was late that evening when Harold and Michael were granted an audience with Sir Thomas Badby. Normally, he would not take visitors at this hour, but the message from Harold briefly explained the urgency of the matter. So a weary Sir Thomas agreed to meet them. Entertaining Her Majesty and organising the welfare of her vast entourage was exhausting and time consuming. He really didn't need to be dealing with such matters at the end of a long, tiring day. But he understood if such a crime had been committed under his roof, he needed to know more and if necessary, take action to apprehend the culprits.

He offered the men some wine, they both declined, this was not a social visit. Michael was in a hurry to find out the progress on finding his daughter's attackers, 'So, Sir Thomas, has this boy Toby and his friends been arrested yet? The longer we leave the search for them, the more likely they will leave Bury.'

A resigned tone in his voice, Sir Thomas confirmed the worst, 'From my initial enquiries I fear the boy Toby may well have already done so. The kitchen servants when questioned by my guards confirmed the assault had taken place in the cellar. They saw him and two other men leaving just before your daughter was found. Little else is known.'

He continued with more unhelpful news, 'Unfortunately, many messengers were sent in advance to the Queen's hosts in Norwich with instructions for her visit. In truth gentlemen, finding this boy was always going to present difficulties. The Queen's entourage numbers over a thousand people, add to that several hundred servants and helpers we draft in, and a young boy like this Toby is easily lost in a small army of unfamiliar faces.'

Harold couldn't contain his anger at this brush off, 'So that's it Sir Harold, just let this rapist get away with it? Is this what the Queen would want, I ask you?'

Sir Thomas bristled at the insolent accusation, 'Sir, I would remind you who you are talking to and words such as those aimed at Her Majesty could result in even more trouble for your family. I will overlook your comments this time, as I understand you are upset and frustrated there is no quick and easy solution in bringing this boy to justice. I am just laying out the facts as they face us. On a positive note, I did inform Her Majesty's guard of this unfortunate occurrence, and they have said they will attempt to find him during their stay in Norwich. If he is caught, he will be brought back here to face justice. That is the best I can do.'

Accepting with that comment, their meeting with Sir Thomas was at an end, Michael and Harold thanked him for his time, and left, still feeling angry at being thwarted in their attempts to find poor Grace's attackers. They arrived back at the house close to midnight, all was quiet, though Robert was still up, wanting to hear the result of their discussions. Over a glass of wine, the three commiserated over the lack of progress and the prospect Toby might escape justice. It soon became apparent to all of them that if Grace's rapist was to be caught and punished, they would have to find him.

Robert at nineteen had developed into a strapping young man, tall and strong, a keen sportsman, his obsession with becoming a first rate swordsman had swelled his muscles and bulked him out. Shaking his hand was akin to putting your hand in a vice. In Harold's opinion, his strength gave him an air of arrogance, an unattractive trait, one which his father seemed blind to, revelling instead in his son's success over opponents in swordsmanship competitions. Now the young man was fired up, anxious to dispense his own brand of justice to his sister's rapists. His father and Harold urged caution, though they understood and sympathised with his desire for revenge. However, as the night drew on, slowly a plan of action came together, one that wouldn't rely on the authorities tracking down and capturing the guilty trio. As Harold said succinctly, 'If you want something done, do it yourself.'

By morning, Robert and Michael were on their way to Norwich.

Chapter 13

Norwich was a two day ride from Bury St Edmunds. By 1578, with a population of 16,000, the city was the second largest, and second wealthiest, in the country. By the time Robert and Michael arrived, the city was finalising preparations for the Queen's impending visit. A frenzy of street cleaning, repairing and burnishing of everything she might possibly set eyes upon was taking place. They made their way to the Bishop's Palace hoping to see the Queen's soon to be host, Bishop Edmund Freke. Not surprisingly he was unavailable, too busy making ready his sumptuous house for the Queen and her senior staff. Looking at the hectic throng of servants and staff buzzing around the Palace, it became depressingly obvious to Robert and Michael that to expect anyone to take the time to seek out and arrest Toby was unlikely—assuming they could even talk to a Justice of the Peace or Sheriff and ask for help. They were all too busy making arrangements for hundreds of guests due to descend upon the city in a few days.

They found an ale house in a street off the large market square. They supped some warm local ale, ate fresh bread, cheese and a leg of chicken. It was their first fulsome meal in two days. They ate out of necessity rather than pleasure. Any feelings of contentment were negated by the slow dawning their visit could be a waste of time. They spent a fruitless day talking to servants, workers, indeed anyone coming in and out of the Abbey asking if they knew of a messenger called Toby. All to no avail.

Michael stopped chewing on his bread and despondently suggested, 'Robert, maybe we should stay the night and then go home? I fear we will achieve little here. Finding this villain would truly be discovering the needle in a haystack.'

Robert's youthful impatience was becoming frustrated at their lack of progress, 'We cannot leave yet Father, we must try for Grace's sake to find this scoundrel. There has to be a way, we just haven't given ourselves enough time.'

'I am as disheartened as you Robert. But we have to be realistic, this is a big city. Everybody is busy wanting to do their best for the Queen's visit, our quest is of no importance to them.'

'Father, we have to do something!' complained Robert, his voicing rising in anger, so much so, one or two of the other patrons glanced nervously in his direction.

'Calm down, son, calm down. Let me ponder on this, see if I can think of a solution.' With that comment, Michael sat back in his chair, ordered another ale, and lapsed into thought.

'Well Father, while you drink your way to a solution, I am going back out to search for that piece of horse shit.' Robert stomped out of the alehouse before his Father could chastise him for his rude remarks. Though he did tell himself the next tankard of ale would be his last for the day.

Robert haphazardly asked almost everyone he met coming from the direction of the Bishop's Palace whether they knew a young messenger by the name of Toby. After more fruitless hours of wandering around, he became increasingly exasperated at everyone's negative replies. Robert then spoke to a guard who unwittingly sowed the seed of an idea in his mind. He hurried back to their lodgings. His Father was napping on a pallet in the corner of the room. He gently woke him up and told him what he had found out.

'Father, I have some interesting news—guess where the Royal Progress goes after it leaves Norwich?'

Still groggy from being abruptly awoken he replied, 'Er...I have no idea. Why? Where?'

'They are going to Hengrave Hall for three nights. Isn't that owned by Sir Thomas Kitson, your cousin?'

'Well, actually he's your Mother's cousin, I know him only vaguely. How does that help us?'

'Think Father, think. Maybe we could ask Sir Thomas's assistance in finding Toby? If we get there well ahead of the Progress we can talk to him. Make a plan of some kind. What do you think?'

His head clearing, Michael began to see the advantage of being ahead of the Progress rather than following it. If they left Norwich today, they could be at Hengrave Hall by tomorrow morning, several days before the multitude arrived.

Michael felt the need to urge caution, even though he felt this might offer a way to catch their target. 'I think it's an excellent idea to pay Sir Thomas a visit, though it has been many years since I last saw him at your Mother's funeral. He is immensely wealthy and has many connections which could prove useful to us in our mission. I hope he remembers who I am! You're right, we have nothing to lose and much to gain. Let us make haste and pray this will be our lucky day.'

They collected the horses from the stables next door to their lodgings and within the hour were trotting through St Stephen's gate heading towards Thetford. Outside of the city walls, long lines of traders were trying to enter, held up by guards collecting taxes on all goods destined to be sold in the market. Following the old Roman road they arrived at Thetford late in the evening, and slept in a barn just south of the town. By noon the following day, they reached Hengrave Hall.

It was a breathtakingly large and handsome stone building, as befitted one of the richest men in the county. It cost an estimated £3,500 to build (over one million pounds in 2023 values) and was said to have included every luxury money could buy: from expensive tapestries and curtains in every room, to mammoth kitchens capable of catering for hundreds of guests.

Sir Thomas Kitson made his fortune as a successful London merchant and invested the proceeds in properties across the county, many former monastic lands. Hengrave Hall was a monument to his wealth and prestige.

Michael and Robert approached the guards at the gates and briefly explained the reason for their unexpected visit. A messenger rode up to the house. After a wait of more than an hour, he returned saying Sir Thomas could spare them a few minutes, but no more.

The ride up the mile long drive meandered through beautifully maintained grassland, kept to a manageable height by dozens of sheep. Huge oak, elm and beech trees provided shade from the August sun. As the Hall came into view, both men stopped for a moment awestruck by its size. It was the largest house the visitors had ever seen. It dwarfed the Abbey buildings in Bury.

'I gather the house has twenty-seven guest rooms,' explained Michael to Robert, adding 'And many of the walls have stone taken from Ixworth Priory. Look over there, they even have their own chapel too! This really is a most impressive residence. I cannot wait to see inside.'

They rode over the moat and were met at the massive front entrance by a perfectly liveried servant. Wordlessly, he led them through the Great Hall, across the large central courtyard, along a hallway lined with paintings and silk wall hangings. Finally, into a large wood panelled room furnished with sumptuous upholstered chairs and a huge table. Sir Thomas was giving orders to some workers. The servant announced Michael and Robert's presence.

He dismissed the workmen, stood up and smiled at his guests. His greeting was warm and welcoming, 'Michael and Master Robert. So good to see you again after such a long time. My, Robert, you are now a strapping young man, when I saw you last at your Mother's funeral, you were but a boy. And Michael you are looking well. Please both take a seat, I am sorry I can spare you only a few minutes. As you know her majesty arrives in a few days, I have much to do to prepare for her visit, and the hundreds who hang onto her coat tails!'

Sir Robert was in his fifties, short and rotund with a florid, plump, but friendly face. He walked stiffly across the room to shake hands and then sat heavily down with a grunt of pain. He explained his gout was particularly bad this morning making walking a painful process. A breeze swept through the room, all the doors and windows were open to keep the August heat at bay. Even so, Sir Thomas looked hot and uncomfortable.

'May I offer you some refreshments?' Both Michael and Robert declined. Sir Thomas ordered some chilled white wine for himself.

'At my age, I find this weather most disagreeable, I only hope it cools down before Her Majesty's visit. Please forgive my directness, but I have a lot of work to do and so little time to finish it. What can I do to assist you?'

'Thank you so much for seeing us, my Lord. We would not be troubling you unless we were in desperate need of your help,' Michael explained.

'Yes, the messenger briefly relayed that your daughter had been assaulted and you think the perpetrator may be coming to my house? I am horrified to hear such news about Grace. Poor child, a terrible thing to have happened. How do you believe I can be of help catching this monster?'

For the next ten minutes, Michael provided Sir Thomas with the gruesome details of Grace's rape, and what they knew of her attackers. That at least one was a messenger in the Queen's entourage, their fruitless chase to Norwich to try and find him, then to discover he may well be part of the Progress arriving at Hengrave Hall in a few days. They had formulated a plan to flush out the villain into the open—however it needed a little help from his Lordship. Appalled at hearing how Grace had suffered, Sir Thomas listened to their plan, made a few suggestions, then without any hesitation, agreed to play his part.

As they stood to leave, Michael was effusive in his thanks, 'Sir Thomas we will be forever in your debt in helping us catch this man. We will come back on the last day of the Queen's stay and put our plan into action. Our sincere thanks, my Lord.'

'I am glad to be of assistance; such acts of barbarity should not go unpunished. I will see you in a few days. Godspeed and good luck.'

As Bury was only a short ride from Hengrave, Michael and Robert returned home to see how Grace was recovering from her ordeal. They entered the house and went straight to her room to find Annette sitting beside her, both looking a lot brighter than a few days earlier.

'You look better daughter, much better, what a relief!' Grace gave her father a wan smile at his announcement, and stood up to hug him, and then her brother.

Annette confirmed her progress, 'She's eating now and has been up and around the house for the past two days, she is much improved I am happy to say. How was your journey... successful?'

Not wanting to divulge too much in front of Grace, Michael merely nodded, adding, 'I will tell you everything this evening my dear. More importantly, Grace seems to be on the mend.' They stayed chatting with her until she was tired, then left her to sleep.

Down in the great hall, Michael retold the details of their trip, the visit to Sir Thomas Kitson, and his willingness to cooperate in finding Grace's attacker. Annette was cautiously optimistic at the news, hopeful that once Grace knew her abuser had been caught, and punished, it would speed her recovery.

The plan to identify and arrest Grace's attacker was deceptively simple, relying on the selfish fact most people like to have their successes recognized. Sir Thomas would reveal to the Queen that one of her vast entourage was a rapist, but picking him out from everyone in the Progress would be impossible without her help. Quite simply, she should announce some games were to be held, solely for the young men in her entourage to find who was the strongest among them. All the young men would be commanded to participate with the hope Toby would show himself-and be arrested. Sir Thomas thought the alternative of asking the Queen's guards to try and find him might give the boy sufficient warning to escape.

Robert and Michael would remain hidden from view while the young men assembled for the games, from whence they could identify him and the arrest take place.

As Sir Thomas predicted, the Queen was most willing to cooperate and help catch '"this despicable scoundrel"' as she called him. So on the last day of the Queen's stay as planned, it was announced that all men under twenty-five should assemble in the huge quadrangle for some games to show off their strength and fitness. While this was being done, the drawbridge would be quietly raised to prohibit any escape attempt.

There was excitement and anticipation as the crowd squeezed into the quadrangle to watch. Nothing like this had happened before on the Progress. What fun! Suddenly, the Queen appeared on a balcony, everyone stopped chattering and knelt until she was seated. One of her guards commanded, 'God Bless the Queen! By order of Her Majesty, any young man under the age of twenty-five, or believes himself to be so, is to form a line in the middle of the quadrangle. The rules of the games will then be announced.'

After a few minutes of pushing and shoving, a line of some twenty young men stood self consciously in front of the Queen and the large crowd. Unused to being the centre of attention, they looked uncomfortable and embarrassed. Michael and Robert peered through a window from a first floor guest room, scanning the line of unknowing suspects. Sir Thomas's head guard stood next to them, 'Do you see the offender sire?" he asked.

'God damn it, he's not there!' swore Michael. 'Could he have suspected a trap?'

'Unlikely sire, only a few people knew of this plan…are you sure he is not there…?'

'Wait!' exclaimed Robert, 'Look, isn't that him now forcing his way through the crowd?'

Michael followed Robert's pointed finger, 'God strewth you are correct son, that is indeed the scumbag.'

The guard asked, 'Are you both absolutely sure he is the boy?'

'Indeed we are!' exclaimed Michael, 'Go quickly to arrest him before he suspects anything.'

Within minutes, a small phalanx of guards pushed their way through the startled crowd. Before Toby could react, they grabbed his arms and dragged him away.

Robert couldn't restrain himself. As murmurings of surprise rose up from the crowd, he leant over the balcony roaring in anger for everyone to hear. Pointing at Toby shouted, 'That man has been arrested for raping my fourteen-year-old sister. He is a vile and evil criminal. I hope he rots in hell for what he did to her!'

The crowd were momentarily stunned into silence by this public accusation. Then seeing Robert's pain and hearing his anguish decided to inflict some instant justice of their own on a now terrified Toby. He pleaded with the guards to protect him as people kicked and beat him with fists, sticks, anything that came to hand. The guards offered him no assistance, seeming to revel in his pain and punishment. By the time Toby was out of the quadrangle on the way to one of Sir Robert's dungeons he was cut, bleeding and bruised.

They unceremoniously threw him onto the cold stone floor and slammed the door, warning him, 'That is just the start of the pain you're going to suffer.'

Sir Thomas shook Michael and Robert's hands, 'The Queen and I are glad we were able to assist in the apprehension of that criminal. I will have him moved to the gaol in Bury St Edmunds where the Justice of the Peace can deal with him.'

Michael bowed as he shook Sir Thomas's hand, 'Thank you so much, my Lord. You have our deepest gratitude for your help. We will be forever in your debt.'

Sir Thomas waved his hand dismissively, 'Think nothing of it. It was a satisfying way to end the Queen's visit. I believe she enjoyed the spectacle too. I am sure justice will now be served.'

It was swift and brutal. Toby, with a little persuasion from the gaolers, revealed the names of his fellow attackers, both local men. Grace bravely confronted the three in court and identified them. They were found guilty on October 6, 1578.

Before a jeering crowd, prior to being hanged, all three were stripped naked and castrated. Their bodies were left hanging all day from the gallows, then taken down and put in gibbets outside the gates of the town for the birds to feast on their remains. A warning to all men such barbaric acts would be met with an equally barbaric end.

Chapter 14

~1608~

Grace awoke to the smell of smoke and the distant cries of people running up the street towards the town centre. She quickly dressed and looked out of her bedroom window, estimating that sunrise was only an hour away. However, the normal pale blue sky over the east side of the town was now mixed with smoke and the red glow of flames darting and curling above the rooftops.

She ran and woke her twin girls, Eve and Marion, signalling them to get dressed immediately and meet her downstairs. Grace gave Marion an extra shake to make sure she was awake. Her deafness made shouting at her totally ineffective. It was a rough way to be woken, but under the circumstances, Grace didn't have time to be subtle. Ignoring their sleep interrupted grumblings, she made it clear without being able to say a word, any delay would not be tolerated. Ten minutes later, all three women left the house and headed up to the Buttermarket and down towards Angel Hill. Before they even reached it, they could smell the smoke, and see the ash and debris from the fire drifting in the air above them. Once there, they witnessed with open mouthed horror the flames attacking the houses along Eastgate Street, and with the aid of a brisk easterly wind, moving quickly towards Northgate Street. Spellbound they watched the rapacious fire consume house after house. Thatched roofs burst into crackling infernos, instantly the wooden beams supporting them were alight. The conflagration was devouring rows of houses as fast as a man could run.

People were dashing towards the fire carrying pails of water in a vain attempt to quell the flames and stop its progress. It was a fruitless exercise. Even from where the three women stood, the searing heat of the fire was in danger of burning their skin. No one fighting the blaze could get close to it without severe injury. They moved back towards Abbeygate street, and safety. Selfishly Grace noticed the wind slightly change direction pushing the fire up Northgate street, Pump Lane and towards the northern part of the town. She prayed it continued in that direction away from their home.

After a few minutes of watching a huge part of the town disappear so quickly in a frightening inferno, Eve nudged Grace and said, 'Mother. There is nothing we can do here. Let us go home and have breakfast. Once the fire has died down we must see what we can do to help anyone who may need a roof over their head.' She tugged at Marion's arm to indicate they were leaving. Marion nodded her understanding and tore herself away from the awe inspiring destruction happening before her eyes.

It took three days before the fire was finally subdued by a heavy downpour of rain. By then it had destroyed one hundred and sixty houses and four hundred outhouses, getting as close as

Woolhall street to Grace's home. Some six hundred people were now homeless. Grace went with Eve, acting as interpreter to the authorities and offered rooms for anyone in need of temporary accommodation.

Later that day there was a knock at the door. Grace's one and only servant opened it to find three women standing there. The eldest asked if this was the house with some rooms to rent? The servant let them into the great hall while she went to inform Grace, Eve and Marion they had visitors.

Eve came down the stairs, smiling, 'Welcome ladies. We are honoured to have you as our guests. Please make yourselves at home.' She directed them to the chairs at the dining room table, 'I am so sorry for the tragedy that has befallen you. It must have been a terrible loss. I hope your stay here will help you recover from such a distressing experience. I am Eve, this is my sister, Marion and mother, Grace. And you are?'

The eldest of the three replied.

'I am Maud, these are my daughters, Joan and Anna. Thank you so much for allowing us to stay with you. Our home in Pump Lane was completely destroyed by the fire. We have only a few possessions to our name. This is a terrible time for us and your help is much appreciated while we decide where our future lies.' She looked around the great hall, 'You have a lovely home Ma'am. It's a privilege to stay here.'

Grace inwardly smiled. It was a genuine compliment, in truth the house was in poor repair. Its upkeep had been a struggle since the death of her father, Michael. Briefly, her brother Robert had maintained it while he tried to start a new business, it failed.

His attempt to become a wool trader floundering as demand and prices dropped. He fled to France in disgrace to avoid his creditors. Many more wealthy than him lost everything as production of finer and more fashionable cloth moved to France and Holland. The East Anglian wool industry had seen its best times. She hadn't seen her brother in years.

That left Grace with two young children to raise and keep the wolf from the door. She never married. The stigma of being raped and the birth of twins as a result, made her an unattractive prospect for any suitor. Her muteness was not a plus point, either. She had made ends meet over the last decade by selling off their landholdings around Bury and taking in the occasional lodger. Now in her forties and with two grown daughters, she was considering opening an alehouse.

In the evening, over a supper of mutton, vegetables and homemade bread, Grace, via Eve, asked what the three women did for a living before their home was destroyed.

Maud, a slim, dark haired woman with piercing blue eyes and a quiet demeanour, replied in a soft voice that was both confident and cultured.

'Our home in Pump Lane was also where we ran a small alehouse. My husband left it to us when he passed away a few years ago. We are, or were, known for our home made pies and extra strong ale!' She was clearly proud of their achievements, adding, 'Men came from far and wide to sample our wares, it was very popular with farmers.'

Grace read between the lines: Two pretty young girls and, she had to admit, a handsome woman close to her age, running an ale house? No wonder it was popular with the male folk! Did they, she wondered, offer other services? Grace mentally scolded herself for thinking such salacious thoughts.

She scribbled on her slate to Eve, 'what do they plan next?' She relayed the question.

Maud replied, 'That is the very problem vexing us at this moment. We have some savings to start again, but we need to find premises. They will be in short supply after the fire I am sure. But do not be concerned Miss Grace, we will be out of your house as quickly as we can find other lodgings and a place to open a new alehouse. We do not plan to outstay our welcome and are happy to pay you rent in the meantime.'

Her quiet, determined attitude impressed Grace. Many women ended up in the workhouse after their husband's death, there were few ways for widows to make an honest living. However, it was Maud's experience in running an alehouse that quietly re-ignited her plans to start a similar venture herself. Maybe there was a potential to work together? Caution dictated she say nothing at the moment until she knew all of them a little better. 'Act in haste, repent at leisure,' as her father said to her on more than one occasion. Advice she wished her brother Robert had heeded. Luckily the house was in Grace's name, safe from his creditors, but by association, her reputation had suffered further. As a result, no lender would advance money for a new venture. A partnership with Maud, if her claims as a successful business woman were true, would be of great help.

She kept her own counsel, only asking Eve through her connections, to find out more about Maud and her daughters. To discreetly enquire about their background, and reputation around the town.

Some days, Grace barely saw her guests. They were out in the town trying to find new premises for their alehouse, or visiting relatives, some of whom had also been made homeless by the Great Fire. When they were in the house, they kept themselves to their rooms in the servant's quarters. However, wanting to play the good host—and to get to know them—Grace organised supper for all of them as often as possible. They were entertaining company. Joan and Anna were of similar age to Marion and Eve and became friends, frequently going for walks together, or playing cards. Neither seemed to find Marion's hard of hearing always a challenge to communication. She was becoming adept at lip reading and could make herself understood, verbally, in a limited way. Her skills at both were improving all the time.

Two weeks after they came to stay, Eve spoke to Grace about them, 'From what I can gather talking to people I know in the town, the family is well regarded. There are some whispers that question why Maud has not remarried. As a successful business owner she would not lack for suitors. Otherwise I can find little about them to cause you concern, Mother.' Grace was relieved. Now the question arose: how to start a discussion of a business partnership?

The friendship grew between Maud and Grace over the ensuing days. Both enjoyed the company of a woman similar in age. Maud patiently accepted conversations could be slow and at times difficult as Grace scribbled replies and questions on her slate. They went shopping to the market together, Maud occasionally acting as interpreter as she became increasingly adept at guessing what Grace wanted to say, but couldn't make herself understood quickly enough. In the evenings, they played cards, read books or just gossiped about people in the town.

One evening, as she was undressing for bed, Grace hit her head on one of the low beams in her bedroom. She managed to stagger to the top of the stairs, blood spilling down her head into her eyes. Before anyone appeared to help, dizziness overcame her and she collapsed.

Grace awoke to see Maud's face close to hers wiping the wound with water, smelling of vinegar and mint.

Maud smiled, holding Grace's hand, 'Quite a bang you gave yourself there my dear. Luckily the wound is not deep and should heal cleanly. I took the liberty of removing your bloody dress and blouse for cleaning.'

Still groggy, Grace blushed as she felt under the bed covers, finding herself now dressed in a nightgown. Maud had seen her naked! She looked for her slate. Maud handed it to her, *'Thank you! maid take over now,'* she scribbled.

'Nonsense,' retorted Maud, squeezing Grace's hand. 'I can tend to you.It is the least I can do after all your kindness. It will give us more time to get to know each other.' She bent over and kissed Grace on the forehead, 'You get some rest. I'll have the maid make some beef broth, I'll bring it up later."

Grace smiled a thank you and watched as Maud left the room, a slight constriction growing in her breast. Just what was she feeling? An emotion unknown, or suppressed was emerging. One buried inside to keep her safe from feeling love, or even becoming too close to someone? She couldn't find the words to describe it. Ever since her rape, men had been an anathema to her, to be feared and hated in equal measure. Now Maud was awakening some previously unimagined feelings. She felt aroused, frightened and bewildered. With these unfamiliar emotions swirling around in her mind, she fell into a deep sleep.

Chapter 15

Maud knew the effect she was having on Grace. She could sense her confusion, reticence, even fear. There was no doubt she found Grace attractive. At forty-five, her girlish looks had not dimmed. Her blonde hair framed a face that was one of a woman twenty years younger. Her striking green eyes still had a spark undimmed by the troubles she had suffered. Maud admired her optimism, independence and determination, undaunted despite her speech impediment. Nevertheless, she understood Grace was in some turmoil and uncertain of her feelings. She was happy to be patient while her new friend decided how she wished to turn her emotions into actions, if at all. Maud had yet to discover why she was unwed, her past seemed cloaked in secrecy, maybe this was the cause of her reticence. No doubt she would find out one day.

Maud had different reasons why her attraction towards men had waned over the years. Her husband had been violent, selfish and lazy. When he died, Maud shed only tears of relief. She took over the alehouse, turning it into a thriving business, but in the process saw again and again the worst side of men. Drunken advances towards her, then Joan and Anna as they grew up and matured into attractive young women. Their violent, and despicable behaviour to the other girls who frequented the alehouse, desperate to earn a few groats by pleasuring the men. Her distaste for the opposite sex grew and deepened as she saw first hand their loathsome manners.

She'd lost all interest in finding another man to replace her husband, deciding life was better without them. Then a young woman called Brenda came to stay. Sensing Maud's antipathy towards men, Brenda befriended, then subtly, slowly, seduced her. Maud put up little resistance to Brenda's advances. At first surprised by the pleasure she derived from another woman's intimacy, Then willingly surrendered to these newly discovered desires with an intensity that consumed her body and soul. Finally, she had found peace and contentment, in the love of another woman.

Brenda moved on, to be replaced with a series of other discreet female lovers. She was astonished to discover how many women had no interest in men. Preferring the gentle, knowing touch of another woman, to the often brutish, selfish and unsatisfying sex men forced upon them.

Two days after her accident, Grace was quietly sitting by the fire in the great room practising her *appliqué*, decorating a large piece of fine cloth. Maud came in and looked over her shoulder, 'My, that is truly beautiful Grace, how long have you been doing appliqué?'

Grace stopped sewing and looked up at Maud smiling at the compliment. She picked up her slate, *'only two yrs still learning.'*

Maud put her hands on Grace's shoulders, 'Well you show exceptional abilities. While I am standing here let me take a quick look at your wound, I want to make sure it is healing cleanly.' She gently parted Grace's hair and inspected the cut. Grace winced slightly at the pain and Maud immediately stopped, 'I am so sorry, I did not intend to hurt you. However, I'm pleased to say the wound is looking healthy. No pus or extrusions.'

Grace reached up and put her hands over Maud's as they rested on her shoulders, squeezing them gently as if to say thank you. Maud looked down at Grace's neck beneath her hairline and couldn't stop the irresistible urge to bend down and gently kiss it. She heard, and felt Grace pull forward catching her breath, then slightly move back, delicately suggesting Maud shouldn't stop. For a minute, Maud gently continued her lips tracing a delicate path down the back and sides of her neck. Grace sighed in pleasure, moaning quietly as Maud's warm, soft touch released a flood of feelings that spread throughout her body.

Maud moved around and knelt in front of Grace, their faces inches apart. She sensed Grace's reluctance, or was it uncertainty, as to what she should do? What should happen next? She slowly leant forward bringing her lips inches from Grace's, waiting to see if she pulled away. For a moment, Grace didn't move, then imperceptibly leant forward, their lips meeting with no more than a tentative brush, then closer, exploring, feeling, tasting. Grace closed her eyes as she was filled with a rush of sensations she'd never felt before. Her uncertainty lasted for only a few seconds before wholeheartedly letting herself be led by Maud into a sensual unknown world that took her breath away.

Grace finally broke away, shaking her head, crying. She hurriedly wrote, 'what we doing? must be wrong?'

Maud gently held Grace's chin, looked straight into her eyes and asked, 'Does it feel wrong Grace? Who are we hurting? No one. Grace you deserve some love, some affection, I can tell you have been starved of it. If you wish me to stop, I will do so, and we will pretend this wonderful moment never happened.'

For a few long moments she stared into Maud's eyes, hers filled with tears of confusion. Then she fell into Maud's arms as relief, joy, and excitement shook her thin body, accepting this was the way it should be.

The next morning, Grace woke to find Maud sleeping beside her. The night had been a journey of sensual exploration. Discovering physical desires she had never experienced. Maud was a skilful and unselfish lover. She led Grace to peaks of passion, pleasure, and moments of tenderness that left her breathless and dazed. She tried to reciprocate and with Maud's gentle guidance found herself exploring another woman's body with fascination and wonder. Way after midnight they both collapsed into a deep, dream free sleep. Exhausted, satisfied and in a world intimacy neither had felt before.

She gently arose from the bed and walked to her table, sat down and started writing a long letter to Maud. For the first time since her attack almost three decades ago, she would put into words what happened, and its effect on her life ever since. Maud deserved to know, and Grace finally had someone who would understand the hurt and hate she had suffered.

For an hour, the quill pen scraped spontaneously across the paper. Grace couldn't write quickly enough to put down the torrent of thoughts and feelings that cascaded from her mind. As she was re-reading her words, she heard Maud awake and pad over to where she was seated.

She nuzzled her neck, then kissed her on the cheek, grinning, she asked, 'Good Morning Grace, I trust you slept well?'

Grace nodded her head and lifted her face towards Maud, silently demanding a kiss on the lips. Maud obliged, then looked down at the table strewn with Grace's writings.

'My, you have been busy. What is it you are putting pen to paper about, if I may ask?'

Grace shuffled the pages into order then thrust them towards Maud, mouthing *'For you.'*

'You wish me to read these?'

Grace nodded her assent.

Maud walked back to the bed and started to read Grace's soul baring letter.

My Dearest Maud,

I shall try and put into words what the last few hours have meant to me, but before doing so, I believe you deserve some knowledge of my previous life in the expectation it will help you understand me, and why I am the person I am today.

I was not always without the gift of speech, an illness as a child robbed me of this God given way to communicate easily with the world. However, I have survived quite well without it, though it is at times like this I wish I could spend hours talking to you, gossiping freely the way women are wont to!

I digress. You asked last night why there is no mention of a father to Marion and Eve? No husband in my life? I choose now to answer your question. I was raped by three men at the age of fourteen. One of them is the father of my daughters. All three were hanged for their bestial crimes long ago. As you can imagine, any attraction I may have towards men died along with those rapists.

Maud stopped reading, horror on her face, 'Grace, Oh my Lord Jesus, you poor woman, what a terrible, terrible ordeal for such a young girl. I am so sorry. Men can be such evil beings... words fail me.'

Grace gently dismissed Maud's sympathy, urging her instead, to keep reading. Maud picked up the letter.

...Of course, though no one would say it to my face, but any prospects I had for a good marriage also died on that scaffold. No man wants a woman who has been defiled in such a way. To this day, I have neither sought the company of a man, nor has one sought mine. I cannot bring myself to even be touched by one.

The only thing that kept me from madness was the birth of my daughters. My Father and Mother were as kind as they could be.

However, there was no escaping the fact they struggled to accept them as true grandchildren and part of our family....

Tears running down her cheeks, Maud struggled to continue reading Grace's cathartic confession. Stopping at times to control her emotions, she just couldn't believe what this beautiful young girl had suffered all these years ago—rape, rejection, a ruined reputation. Despite all of it, she remained positive, raising two beautiful and confident daughters. She continued to read.

...I won't test your patience with the trials my daughter's and I have faced over the years. My brother's failed business, his fleeing to France, yet another black mark against our family name. It would make for tedious reading and, in truth, painful for me to write.

So our lives continued, seemingly from one tribulation to the next. Numbly existing day-to-day. Then the Great Fire, and the day you and your daughters arrived at our house. I knew, deep down, the moment you entered our home my life would change forever. Of course I never dreamt it would be this way! At the time, I did not realise the profound way your companionship, the way our friendship, would blossom in the beautiful manner it has. I am not sure what the future holds for us. But one thing of which I am sure, you have awakened desires and feelings within my heart I could have never foreseen.

What has just happened between us has lifted my spirit and gladenned my heart in ways I have not felt since the birth of my daughters. The feelings you have unleashed within me defy my limited capacity to explain when putting ink to paper. Inside I am a maelstrom of excitement, passion and gratitude. Even if we are to never repeat what took place last night (though I sincerely hope and wish we do!) I will be forever grateful for your kindness and for making me feel like a woman again.

With love, I am forever in your debt,
Grace.

Maud dropped the papers onto the floor by the bed. Teary eyed, she beckoned Grace over to lie beside her. With no words spoken, they lay together so close as to be one, oblivious to time, the only sound, their hearts seemingly beating in rhythm together.

Chapter 16

~1610/11~

'Out! Out! You drunken old fart!' Maud shouted as she unceremoniously pushed the last customer out of the tavern. She turned to Grace who was cleaning the tables, while Marion tidied up behind the bar.

'Good Lord! That was a busy evening ladies! I am exhausted. Let us finish here quickly, my bed is calling me.' Both Grace and Marion wearily agreed. As they went upstairs, Grace made sure to gather up the evenings' takings, she would count them tomorrow. It was a substantial amount, as it had been each evening for many weeks. Finally, after months of planning and expense the the tavern in Grace's house was starting to make money.

It had taken forever to get a licence from the Justice of the Peace, it was only granted because of Maud's reputation as a successful alehouse owner, convincing him it would not become a *house of ill repute*.

The next hurdle was money. No money lender was prepared to help them. They were all wary of supporting a business run wholly by women. So Grace invested her remaining savings and combined with the money Maud made from her previous alehouse, they had enough to open *The Gentlemen's Rest*, in time for Christmas 1609. They deliberately chose to open as a tavern selling wine and food, rather than only ale. 'It will attract a more upper class customer.' Maud assured Grace. And she had been proved right.

The great hall became the main bar room, a welcoming fire burning continuously in the huge inglenook fireplace. The furnishings were the best quality they could afford, comfortable chairs with matching tables. Booths were built for privacy along one wall. Every Friday and Saturday, they would have musicians playing. They even allowed gambling. 'It will make customers stay longer and drink more,' suggested Maud. They discouraged working girls from entering the tavern, as they felt it would cause trouble and attract undesirable characters.

Upstairs, in the south wing, in what had once been the servants' rooms, three were converted for lodgers. Each was furnished for a maximum of four occupants. A fourth room, especially lavish, with rugs on the floor, and a comfortable bed with curtains round it for privacy and warmth, was rented out at a premium rate of a shilling a night. The rooms were all let tonight so Grace made sure the doors to their bedrooms in the north wing were locked and bolted—preventing unwanted male visitors from making a nuisance of themselves.

Grace deposited the bag of coins in the lockbox in the corner of her bedroom. She hesitated, mentally tallying up the amount stored there, more than twenty-five pounds, she estimated. Equal to three working men's yearly wages—and all made in just a few months. She thought it was time to sit down with Maud and decide how to invest it in the tavern, or possibly some other property. A discussion for another day, she was too tired to think about such weighty matters at this time of night. By the time she had washed and undressed, Maud was already in bed, waiting for her. For nearly two years, that beautiful sight had awaited her every night. Grace never failed to get excited at the thought of another night in Maud's arms. They had become inseparable, first lovers then business partners. Living for each other every hour of the day, caring, sharing, giving, everything was done with the other in mind. Grace had never felt so alive, so wanted, so full of purpose.

What pleased her equally was the acceptance of their relationship by all their daughters. They all knew the unsettling history of their Mothers at the hands of brutish men. If they had found love and happiness with another woman, so be it. Others outside of the family might question it, gossiping, making malicious comments, but she and Maud ignored it and became oblivious to the pernicious whispers. They had each other, that was all they needed.

Grace slid into the bed beside the now drowsy Maud. She mimed 'I love you,' Maud responded by kissing her gently on the lips. They lay down in each other's arms. In the moments before sleep overtook her, Grace's only regret was the hard work of running the tavern had curtailed their love making. An act of physical and emotional conjunction she still found wildly exciting and satisfying after all this time. No matter, not for the first time she counted her blessings, grateful for the love of a kind and compassionate woman.

*****

It was Christmas 1611, *The Gentlemen's Rest* was celebrating its second anniversary. The business had thrived to such an extent, that in a week's time, on January 1st 1612, Maud and Grace would open their second establishment, *The Abbey Tavern*, on Angel Hill, in a building where the monks once brewed beer before the Abbey was destroyed. It took a year to renovate and was twice the size of *The Gentlemen's Rest*. Maud's daughter Joan and her new husband, John, would run it. They had also invested in a small farm in the village of Lawshall, where Grace's daughter Marion and her husband David, would grow produce and keep livestock to supply the two taverns, selling any excess at the weekly market in Bury. The farmhouse had been built a few years earlier and was in the same village as Coldham Hall where Sir Robert Rookwood lived and Lawshall Hall where William Drury was said to have entertained Queen Elizabeth 1st on her Royal Progress of 1578. The farm had about fourteen acres of arable land, more than enough to produce food for both tavern's needs.

One cold Sunday in February, Grace and Maud went to visit the farm, and see how David and Marion, now expecting their first child, were settling in. The small house was one of the first to have a brick chimney, allowing for a second floor to be built, doubling the amount of living space. Still, with only two ground floor and two first floor rooms, compared to the house in Whyting street, it was small, basic and sparsely furnished. No expensive floorboards—just a bed of straw covering the floor, unwhitewashed walls, and shutters, not glass, to cover the windows. But with a roaring fire in the huge inglenook fireplace (large enough for them to actually sit beside the fire) it was cosy and warm.

As they all chatted over a fine meal prepared by Marion, the young couple were still full of enthusiasm for their new home. David was particularly happy with his lot. A large man, with a mop of curly black hair that continued round into a massive bushy beard framing his perpetually smiling face and ruddy red cheeks. A farmer all his life, he was thrilled to now be working his own land, not the Lord of the Manor's, as he'd previously done in nearby Hawstead. He was determined to make this new venture a success.

As he slurped down some rabbit stew and fresh bread, he outlined his plans for the farm, 'We're putting about ten acres aside for grazing cows and sheep. Then the remainder, nearest the house, for vegetables and fruit trees. Oh, and of course, chickens!'

'When do you hope to start planting?' asked Maud.

'The last frost is normally late March, so soon after that. Buying the seeds has been expensive; we cannot afford to waste any. We're lucky the farmer across the way says we can have some hay for the animals if we help him at harvest time.'

'And what do you hope to grow?'

'We will try cabbages, onions, cauliflower, cucumbers, and leeks, to start with. We would like to try and grow this new vegetable I heard about called a potato? Have you seen it?'

Maud nodded her head, 'That is from the Americas I gather? I have seen one seller in the market offering it. He says it is easy to grow. It would make an interesting addition to our menu at the taverns. If I see them again I will buy some for you.'

The conversation continued, Marion able to contribute more and more as her lip reading skills had improved immeasurably. At times, thought Grace, it would be hard to tell she was almost totally deaf. It was, she often pondered, a strange coincidence that two women born in the same house should have afflictions of the head.

She had no way of knowing the dark secret within the house that caused such debilitations. Even after a century, the old witch's conjurations were still working.

By three in the afternoon, it was already gloomy outside. Maud and Grace bade their farewells and rode the seven miles back to Bury before it was completely dark. They did not open on a Sunday, so the evening was a time to relax, play cards, read, or in Grace's case, write her regular letter to Maud. At least once a week and sometimes more frequently, she put down on paper her concerns, ideas and always, always her love for Maud. She'd use the opportunity to outline her plans for the future asking Maud's advice about them. It was an easier way to communicate weightier matters, ones that needed more thought and discussion. In addition, it allowed Grace to keep a permanent record of her life with Maud. Something she could look back on in the future, a reminder of the wonderful times living with a strong, loving woman.

Living together for two years, they developed a shorthand both verbal and written that guided them efficiently through day to day conversations, but these letters enabled Grace to raise matters that needed a more considered deliberation. Maud looked forward to reading them, they were an insight into Grace's thinking, and always full of considered and thoughtful advice about the business. Having discussed their contents and answered any question's Grace had raised, she carefully saved the letters. Already one trunk was full with such correspondence. Maud in her spare moments, loved re-reading the older ones, they were not just a diary of how their business had changed and developed, but their relationship as well.

There were times when Maud wondered if customers would ever question the close friendship of two women. In the past, she heard the occasional lewd comment such as *strumpet* whispered at her by a drunken customer, otherwise little was said. Many taverns were run by women, so to see two of middle age in such a business arrangement was unusual, but not rare. There were always other women around, helping behind the bar, in the kitchen, serving, which helped conceal that she and Grace shared a house and bed.

*****

Both taverns continued to prosper for close to a decade. The farm in Lawshall proved fertile and an excellent source of produce—including potatoes. More land was bought and the farm became a source of considerable profit for the family.

Children from all four daughters were born in quick and numerous succession, so that by the end of 1621 Maud and Grace had nine grandchildren between them. Then came a shock —Eve and her husband Peter, a carpenter, decided to seek a new future in the Americas as were many in East Anglia at that time. They departed in 1623 on the ship *Anne,* bound for Plymouth, Massachusetts. Grace was heartbroken, she couldn't understand what the attraction was in travelling to an unknown land, risking your life in the process.

Eve, who had become a fervent Puritan, tried to explain, 'Mama, we are finding it difficult to practise our religion here, our beliefs are increasingly attracting ridicule, threats and violence. The New World is a free land where we can do and say as we please. And worship without fear. We are being offered free land in return for Peter's skills. We feel we have no choice but to take this opportunity.'

Grace offered to buy them some land in Norfolk, but they were adamant. When her final plea to stay had been refused by the young couple, Grace bowed to the inevitable and gave them a generous sum of money to ensure they didn't start their new life in debt, as so many did.'She is as wilful and stubborn as me,' admitted Grace to Maud days before their departure.

They held a small farewell party at *The Gentlemen's Rest.* It was a sombre affair, their tightly knit family was breaking up. Days later the whole family watched tearfully as Eve, Peter and their young daughter departed early in March 1623 for Harwich on the east coast. All knew it was unlikely they would ever see them again. Though it wasn't unheard of for those who did not pull their weight in the Colonies to be sent back to England.

171

Grace knew Eve and Peter would prove hard working members of the fledgling communities in that far off land, and make a new, successful home for themselves.

As the 1620s came to a close, Maud and Grace agreed that Anna, and her husband Charles, should take over the running of *The Gentlemen's Rest*. They were now entering their sixth decade. The numerous business interests they started were now proving too burdensome for their age. The work was divided up among the daughters and their husbands to manage. They owned several houses in Bury and two other farms near Rougham. They wanted to end their years enjoying the fruits of twenty year's hard work. Maud and Grace retired to one of their other homes in Whyting street, just a few doors down from the Tavern.

Their retirement was short, Grace caught pneumonia in the severe winter of 1633 and died on Christmas Eve. The illness was punishingly swift in taking her. As she lay in her bed, painfully short of breath Maud sat holding her hand. Grace indicated she wanted to write something on her slate, but lacked the energy to even sit up. In frustration she tossed it onto the floor.

'It matters not Grace, we have said everything that needs to be said. You know I love you more than life itself. You have been my steadfast friend and lover for over twenty years. If I had my life over again, I would never find the likes of you. I thank the Lord for the day we met and have not regretted a single one thereafter...I know you feel the same way too. I do not envy all the others, for they will never know how fortunate we have been. You have poured out your heart to me in your letters, which I will treasure and read again and again. You will be forever with me because of them.'

172

Grace squeezed Maud's hands, smiled weakly and fell to sleep. Later that day, when she came in to see if Grace needed anything, she was gone, her face in death, serene and still beautiful. Lying on her breast was her slate. She had somehow found the strength to retrieve it from the floor and write her last words:

'You have been my everything. I am blessed to have loved you. See you in heaven my angel. G.'

Distraught at Grace's death, the normally resilient Maud slowly lost interest in everything around her—the business, her family, the world outside. Without her life partner, she was mentally and physically untethered, drowning in a sea of grief.

Two weeks after Grace's funeral, talking to Marion she broke down, 'We were inseparable while we lived, like two parts of an unbreakable whole. Now Grace is gone I feel my heart has been ripped from me. There is a void inside that cannot be filled. I wonder just what purpose I have left on this earth when I know my Grace is waiting for me.'

Marion and the whole family attempted to comfort the heartbroken Maud. Trying to install a spark of life back into her. They brought the grandchildren to play more frequently, and visited her several times a week. But her malaise worsened. After dining with Maud one evening, Anna recounted the visit to her husband, 'She has lost the will to live, Charles. She takes no interest in anything except reading those letters that Grace wrote to her. I know not what to do to bring her *joie de vivre* back. Her body and mind are wasting away.'

Charles sat down beside her, 'Anna, all you can do, any of us can do, is be with her as much as we can. Grief is a terrible master. You either break out of its control and continue your life, or you submit to its weight, its leaden grasp of helplessness, and succumb to a life of misery. Only your mother can make that choice.'

With resignation and pain, the family watched Maud let the loss of Grace overwhelm her. It became clear she had lost the will to live. She was dying of a heart broken in two, one part forever lost with Grace's death. Two months after her loss, Maud returned to *The Gentlemen's Rest* to stay for a few days. With difficulty, she pried open a small section of the wood panelling in her room to reveal where she and Grace had kept the tavern's strong box. She gathered up as many of Grace's letters as she could fit into it, firmly padlocked the lid, then replaced the section of panelling. No one would notice, the fit was so perfectly crafted.

Two days later, Anna came into Maud's room with breakfast. She dropped the tray and screamed for Charles.

Maud lay dead on her bed. Her face a study of repose and peace. In death the grief and sadness that had ravaged her in the weeks since Grace's death had gone. They both walked over to her body and Charles picked up a note she had died holding in her hand.

The message simply said: '*I have gone to have my heart made whole again.*'

Chapter 17

~1637~

The Bubonic Plague, or Black Death, repeatedly devastated the country's population since 1347. It again swept into Bury in the spring of 1637. It wasn't the first time the great pestilence had visited the town, the years 1349, 1539 and 1589 hall saw hundreds die each time it appeared. No one understood its cause, so nothing could be done to prevent its spread. Daily the accumulation of dead bodies grew. Then as quickly as it arrived it, too, died leaving a depleted and frightened township, left to rebuild itself.

The latest epidemic was by far the worst. Tents were set up outside the town walls to try and isolate those infected, it proved ineffectual. By July of that year, the number of dead in Bury tripled from the previous month, to over 100. August and September saw the number reach over 160. By the time the worst had passed, the town had been closed down for almost nine months. Over ten percent of the population had died, in excess of six hundred souls.

As the Plague rampaged through the town, businesses were closed, boarded up, many never to reopen. People huddled inside their houses, too scared to emerge into streets that carried the dead each day to mass graves outside the town. Many starved to death as their food ran out. At *The Gentlemen's Rest*, Charles and Anna, Joan and John were like the rest of the population: in quarantine. It was August, both their taverns had been closed for three months. Whatever food they had stored was running low. They were discussing the idea of all moving out to the farm to stay with Marion and David.

'When was the last time you saw them?' asked Charles.

Joan thought for a second then replied, 'I think it was round Easter? They were all well at that time. I have heard nothing since. We had our last delivery of vegetables in June but they were brought by one of their gardeners. Before we all go there, we need to find out if they are well and able to accommodate us.

John agreed, suggesting, 'I shall ride there early tomorrow to ascertain their health and willingness to help us.'

Joan held up her hand in warning, 'John, that is a dangerous trip. The Alderman has made it plain people should not travel for fear of spreading the pestilence. They have closed all the town's gates to stop anyone leaving or entering the town. You could be arrested if caught.'

'You are right Joan, but what is the alternative? We cannot just arrive at your sister's without warning? I will leave before sunrise and take great care not to be seen by anyone in authority. There is an old trail down by Fryers Lane, it will take me up to the

Hardwicke Estate, and thence on the road to Lawshall. I know Sir Robert Jury, he is a regular in our tavern, he will not mind me waiting there until nightfall when I return.'

John left the stables in Guildhall street as the sun was coming up. It was just after five o'clock. As he crossed Westgate street to Fryers lane, he saw two carts heading towards the Risby gate, their ghastly cargo of bloated corpses covered in pustules and boils making their final irreverent journey to a communal grave at St Peter's Pit. John nodded to the men, swaddled head to toe in cloth as protection against the pestilence, they ignored him. He was soon on the road weaving past Nowton Hall heading towards Hawstead. He saw only a farm worker or two solitarily working the fields. Soon it would be harvest time and John wondered if there would be enough people to bring the crops in before they rotted away, worthless. As far as he could see, the fields were ready, broad swathes of yellow, golden and all hues in between as the barley, wheat and oats ripened in the warm August sun. Under normal circumstances, it would be a sight to warm any farmer's heart. However, if the manpower was lacking, it would all be for naught.

He passed Coldham Hall, its majestic long gravelled drive leading up to the huge house recently built by Sir Robert Rookwood. The solid metal gates were locked to deter any visitors. A mile further along on the right he saw Marion and David's small farmhouse. The omens were not good. No smoke was coming from the chimney and in the yard behind the house he could see several dead chickens and a dog's carcass.

He tied his horse to the fence and nervously walked up to the open back door, shouting a welcome.

There was no response. He covered his mouth with a kerchief and entered the kitchen. It was ransacked, as, he discovered, was the rest of the house. What little furniture they had was broken and strewn around the room. He searched the house, then went outside, passed the small barn, and walked into the fields. The cattle and sheep seemed in good health, their water troughs full. Puzzled, he walked back up to the track which passed along the front of the farm and into the village, seeking someone who might provide information on what had happened.

John found a neighbour tending to his vegetables, and from a safe distance asked, 'Sir, do you have news of Marion and her husband David? I see their farm is deserted.'

The man looked up, suspicion on his face, and asked, 'And who might you be, sir?'

'I am Marion's brother by marriage, John, we run the tavern in Bury called *The Gentleman's Rest,* they provided us with food and meat. I am anxious to ascertain their health and whereabouts.'

Leaning on his hoe, the man sighed, 'Tis not good news sir. They fell for the pestilence some four, no five weeks ago. I believe one of their gardeners brought it back after a visit to the town. The priest buried them in the village graveyard. Their two children are with another family in the village. The Coopers at the farm of the same name just up the road yonder. I am sorry to bear such gloomy tidings, sir.'

John was stunned. The whole family were sure living out here would be safe from the pestilence. By sheer bad luck it had

178

proved not to be the case. There would be much upset when he imparted the sad news to everyone this evening.

'Sir, the cattle and sheep seem in good health, are you looking after them?'

The man nodded, 'Yes sir. They are valuable, I would hate to see them die for the want of some water. It is no problem. I may take one for food at some time with your permission? I am sorry I was unable to stop some local rogues stealing anything of value in the house.'

John replied, 'You have done more than enough, Please take one of the animals sir, it is a fair payment for your time and effort. I will be back in a few days with Marion's sister, once we have decided what to do with the farm. I owe you a debt of gratitude for being such a good neighbour.'

The man waved a hand as if to say it was no bother and went back to his weeding.

He fetched his horse and found Coopers Farm some two hundred yards down the lane from the Farm. He approached the small house, badly in need of repair to its roof and shutters. He cautiously announced his arrival. A young, harassed looking woman with a baby perched on her hip warily opened the door.

'Good day to you Ma'am, I am John, my relatives owned the farm down the road. I understand you are caring for their children as their parents passed recently from the pestilence?'

Wearily, she opened the door a little wider and before she could answer, two young girls rushed out, 'Uncle John!' they cried in unison as they ran up to his horse.

He dismounted, bent down and hugged them, 'Hello Jane, hello Diane, it is so good to see you my little ones.' Unsure what to say about their parents, he looked up at the woman still standing in the doorway. 'What have you told them, Ma'am?'

'I had to tell them the truth, sir. I had no choice. I am unsure if they truly understand what has happened. They seem happy enough in themselves I reckon. Quite a handful at times I have to admit.' With a brusqueness that shook John, she promptly asked, 'So you'll be taking them with you?'

John hesitated for a moment, 'Er...Ma'am this tragic news has caught me unprepared. Could I ask for your help, and keep them for a few more days? I shall be returning to sort out arrangements for the sale of the farm.'

The woman looked reluctant, 'I have little enough food for my own family, two extra mouths to feed is a great burden sir.'

John quickly saw what was expected of him, 'Please, let me give you some coins as recompense.' Without a second's delay, the woman's hand shot out in front of her. John deposited three shillings into her filthy hands.

Suddenly, she was all smiles, 'That is most kind of you, sir. I shall take good care of them for a few more days only, I have three of my own. I cannot manage these extra two for much longer.'

180

'I am grateful Ma'am for your help in these difficult times, I shall return before the week's end.'

He bent down and hugged his two nieces again, promising them he would be back soon and to behave themselves in the meantime. They promised to do so and looked at him tearfully as he mounted his horse.

The elder, Jane, pleaded, 'You will come back soon won't you Uncle John?'

'Of course, I will. I promise, it will be in a day or two.'

They waved him goodbye as he rode back through the village towards Bury. He was in a melancholy mood. It had been a terrible blow hearing of Marion and David's deaths. Even worse, he now had to impart the devastating news to the rest of the family.

It was late in the evening, everyone was still digesting the appalling account of his visit to the farm. What to do next? Sell the farm? Undoubtedly, at a low price, the pestilence had crushed land values. Should one family move there? Or indeed should they all go? Aside from the four adults, they had three children each. Could the little farmhouse accommodate twelve people, including the orphaned nieces? If they all moved to Lawshall, what should they do with the two closed taverns in Bury? They agreed to sleep on it and make a decision the following day.

The next morning they were all in agreement, taking the view that staying at the house in town while the pestilence raged in the all around them was too much of a risk. They had no idea how long it would last. Being imprisoned in your own home for months to come was an unappealing prospect, especially with six children. The decision was made to board up the house and both families move to Lawshall. They would go from being inn keepers to farmers and return when the pestilence was finally spent.

Within three days, they packed up their belongings, piling them onto two carts. They stopped in Lawshall to collect Jane and Diane and all squeezed into the tiny farmhouse. Relieved to be away from the misery and horrors they experienced every day in Bury.

They would never live in the Whyting street house again. The following year, Anna and Charles, joined six hundred other Suffolk residents and made the one way trip to Virginia in the Americas. It was prescient timing. Suffolk's economy was in the doldrums as the cloth and wool industry collapsed in the face of demand for finer products they couldn't, or wouldn't, manufacture. A demand fulfilled by suppliers in France, Belgium and Holland. It would never recover.

The houses and taverns in Bury were sold. Wisely, Maud and Grace had no loans against them, allowing for Anna and Charles to depart to the New World with a substantial amount of money.

Joan and John remained, at what they now called West Farm. Adopted Jane and Diane, making five children in the family. Enlarged the farmhouse, to accommodate them all, bought extra land, and became successful farmers.

*****

The house stood empty while the new owner, a landlord, Tobias Davenport, of dubious standing, ripped out all the valuable furnishings including the beautiful wood panelling in the great room and sold them at auction. Even some of the glass windows were removed for sale.

The larger rooms downstairs and in the north wing, once the owner's accommodation, were divided up for lodgers or those who needed to rent cheap accommodation.

He cared little for the damage done to the house by his indifferent tenants and guests, leaving them un-repaired until it was absolutely necessary for something to be made good.

Over the three years it was used as a lodging house, it became known as a refuge for women cast out by their families when they became pregnant out of wedlock. The dingy, dirty rooms saw many women give birth in the most squalid conditions. But it was not the risk of disease or illness which showed itself among the newborn. With alarming frequency the children were afflicted with conditions affecting their hearing, speech or sight.

Midwife Maggie Dowling in attendance at many of the births was not one to spread rumours. Her occupation required her to be discreet and private, but even she began to wonder if the house had some kind of curse upon it. Nowhere else did she see so many babies with similar conditions.

'Tis most strange and worrisome,' she complained to her husband Jonathan one day. 'To see so many babies born with such terrible maladies, it is most upsetting. Some mothers ask me to put their newborns out of their misery on discovering they have such problems. I cannot do it, but I know some that have done so. Who can blame them? Their babies are already destined for a life of strife and poverty, if they cannot talk or see, what future do they have?'

Her face reflected the pain and suffering she saw every day. She was supposed to help bring joy and healthy babies into the world. Instead, at this strange house, many arrived with the most terrible deformities. Her husband tried to comfort her, 'It is not your fault dearest. I am not superstitious but it seems that the house is cursed with bad luck for children and babies. I remember the previous owners, many years ago. The mother was unable to talk and one of her daughters was deaf.'

Tobias Davenport's indifference to the condition of the house and its upkeep, finally caught up with him when one of the ceilings collapsed, killing two lodgers and injuring many others. Unable, or unwilling to pay for the repairs, he evicted all the tenants and left the house empty. It was a year later the fine old house was purchased by someone with enough money to restore it to its former glory.

Unfortunately, for the new owner, no matter how much he lavished on repairing the house, its dark secrets still remained to torment its future occupants.

Chapter 18

~1642~

The English Civil Wars comprised of three wars, which were fought between Charles I and Parliament between 1642 and 1651. The human cost was devastating. Up to 200,000 people lost their lives, or 4.5 percent of the population. The causes of the wars were complex. At the centre of the conflict were disagreements about religion, and discontent over the king's use of power and his economic policies.

It is 1642, a year in English history never to be forgotten. The country is at war with itself. This time it is not warring families fighting for the throne. It is the King versus his own government. Parliament is unhappy with King Charles 1st's excesses, and his belief he is the ultimate ruler of the kingdom, guided by God's hand. Finally, as he continued to ride roughshod over the elected assembly of MP's, they moved to curb his excesses. Over the ensuing months and years, the country would become divided into the Royalists supporting the King and the Parliamentarians (later to become known as the Roundheads).

'It is a sorry state in which we find ourselves. Neighbour fighting neighbour, families ripped apart as they take different sides in this argument. Where will it end?' asked a bemused Henry Jermyn. He was talking to Sir William Castleton, the high Sheriff of Suffolk in the great hall of his new house in Whyting street. He bought the property from an unscrupulous landlord who allowed the house to fall into serious disrepair. It had been empty for a year and was in need of much work. Henry knew the house was well over one 150 old, and aside from a new tiled roof to replace the thatched one after the Great Fire of 1608, little had been done to update it. He had spent considerable sums turning it back to a home after its use as tenements. Now just as he was enjoying a position of wealth and prestige, the country, every county and town was in turmoil. His normal bombastic and expansive self was much subdued today.

Sir William nodded his head in agreement, 'You are right, Henry. It is tragic for all of us. Unfortunately as I was just appointed by the King, I fear suspicion will befall me, branding me a Royalist. When in truth, I have no affiliation either way. The Parliamentarians have made a good argument to curb the King's excesses, but the manner in which they press their claims will cost many lives. The Corporation here is strongly aligned with Parliament, I hear they are trying to recruit men for their cause. I will have to decide soon which side to support.'

'What will you do?' asked Henry. He, too, was unsure which side to champion. The town and county were in the main favourably disposed to supporting Parliament. A few aristocratic stalwarts were ready to defend the King, but not many. Remaining neutral was not an option, Sir William took a drink from his tankard and thought for a moment. A distinguished looking man, tall, well dressed, with greying hair and a slight stoop, today, he no longer looked like a man in control of his own destiny. His confident air shaken by claims of his Royalist connections. He didn't answer Henry's question, instead, changing the subject, he looked around the great hall.

'You have done a fine job at restoring this house Henry. I remember coming here when it was a tavern, run by two women if I recall correctly. Served good food and fine wine. Damn shame that pestilence caused it to close.'

'Thank you, Sir William. Yes, I occasionally frequented the establishment too.' Laughing, he reminisced, 'After one too many glasses of wine I tried to bed one of them, the mute one I think. Lovely looking woman, but she rebuffed me in no short order. I heard whispers that the two of them preferred each other's intimacy to that of a man's.'

Sir William laughed, 'Really? Well they kept that well hidden! Talking of ladies, I hear you have found yourself a new young wife?'

'Indeed I have and she is already with child. My previous wife, God rest her soul, proved incapable of providing a son to keep my family name alive. My dearest Louise has obliged me quickly in that department. I hope it will be a boy.'

Sir William finished his glass of wine and stood up to leave, 'Henry on that good news I will wish you and your wife well. Now I must return to the court to see what plans are being hatched behind my back! I gather they are intending to move the magazine and powder to a safer place. I believe they think I will use it to help the Royalist cause. I fear the fence upon which I currently sit is about to collapse under the weight of my indecision!'

After Sir William left, Henry eased himself out of his comfortable chair and once more decided to walk through the house to see what else could be done to make it comfortable for his wife and new child. He had already hired a nursemaid, which, in addition to the cook and two servants meant most of the southern wing of the house was full. The huge kitchen, buttery and pantry took up the downstairs. There were four rooms on the second floor for the servants and the large attic space on the third floor was used for storage.

He wondered if he should dig out a cellar for his wine and use it as cold storage for food, but that would be expensive and disruptive—not to be done with a young mother and baby in the house.

The newly decorated great hall, with the large fireplace connected to the north wing, in layout a copy of the south wing. Their bedroom and the next door room, now a nursery, took up the entire ground floor, upstairs were guest rooms, his study and more storage. It was a big house for a family of three, he hoped more children would come along to help fill it. Already in his late forties, Henry was aware that time was not on his side to start a big family, but one on the way was a wonderful start.

As one of the top lawyers in Bury, he was kept busy, dealing mainly with disputes between merchants and aristocrats squabbling over loans or land rights. He envisaged the developing civil war leading to many trials for treason and sedition, it would be good for business! Though he would have to keep his allegiance discreet. Thankfully, as a lawyer, impartiality was expected of him, and he hoped that extended to his views on the civil strife engulfing the country.

From his meetings with the gentry of Suffolk as far as Henry could tell, most were neutral while the poorer folk sided with the Parliamentarians or 'Roundheads' as they were known. He was aware that a new organisation set up by the Roundheads, called The Suffolk County Committee was due to meet with the objective of raising funds and an army to support them. They would not have it all their own way, a significant number of the gentry were still supporters of the King—especially those at the receiving end of his *largesse*.

Throw into this simmering pot of hostility the inflammatory and contrary demands of papists and puritans meant the county was set to boil over at the slightest provocation. Too close for Henry's comfort was the recent sacking and despoliation of his friend the Countess of River's home at Long Melford for her papist beliefs. Her fine hall was reduced to ruins by a mob of several hundred Protestants.

As he sat by the fire, mulling over the problems facing his town and country, he heard Louise come slowly down the stairs from her afternoon rest. She was due to give birth at any time, Henry marvelled at the way she carried the baby inside her with such ease and grace. She had rarely complained, and luckily had not suffered from any sickness during her pregnancy—a sign he was assured that the child would be fit and healthy.

'Please sit here my dear, you look tired. Would you like some refreshments?' As he asked the question, he heard a commotion

189

out in the street. The sounds of horses hooves on the cobblestones, people shouting, windows being smashed, mayhem right outside their front door!

'Stay here my dear, let me find out what is going on.' He went out onto the street and saw a raucous crowd coming towards him. They were knocking on people's doors, and in some cases throwing rocks through their windows.

Henry shouted at one of the rioters and asked what was going on? From the far side of the street a man came over wielding a large cudgel. Henry saw he was drunk and fired up, ready to cause trouble.

Slurring his words, he waved his cudgel menacingly in the air, 'We are here to expose any Royalists so we may come back to them later when the Roundheads have prevailed. Who do you support sir? Are you for the King or with Cromwell?' The man poked his cudgel in Henry's face, demanding an answer. Henry guessed the men were for Cromwell, the leader of the Parliamentarians. The common folk had little love for the King after years of tax increases and indifference to their suffering.

Henry tried a non committal answer, 'I have yet to make up my mind on this matter, both sides....'

Before he could explain further, the man leant close to him, his wild eyes flickering with hate, 'Tis no time to be lily livered sir, you must choose one side or t'other. Which is it to be?'

By this time, a crowd had gathered around the man, chanting 'Roundheads! Roundheads! Let's have the King's Head!"

190

Henry knew he couldn't talk or reason his way out of this argument. All his lawyerly skills were for nothing at this moment. As he vacillated before replying, he heard his wife's voice.

'Enough of your threats!' She pushed past him and confronted the rabble in front of the house. 'I and my husband's beliefs are our own to reveal when we wish to. If you want to attack us, do so. I am with child as you can see. What would your wives and daughters say if they found out you injured a pregnant woman? If you were my husband I would scold you til your ears burned! I am sure your fate might be worse should you injure me. So be off with you and leave peaceful people alone. You should be ashamed of yourselves!'

Confronted by an irate pregnant woman, the crowd were shaken into an embarrassed silence. The cudgel wielding man doffed his hat and muttered some apologies. He turned to the others and ordered them to move on. Begrudgingly, they turned and walked towards Westgate street, the wind taken out of their sails by Louise's brave words.

Henry stood for a moment flabbergasted at her gall, her spirit. It was a side of her he had never seen before. After a few moments, he gathered his wits and led Louise back into the house, sat her down and summoned a servant to bring some wine to calm their nerves. The realisation of how reckless her actions were, and the danger she had put herself in, soon asserted itself and she sat pale faced, shivering in shock.

Henry took her hand, 'My dear Louise, what were you thinking? You and our child could have been injured. It was reckless, though very brave of you to confront those ragamuffins.

I am so proud of you. How are you feeling now? You look a little…shaken?'

Louise didn't reply, she rocked gently back and forth, holding her stomach. She sipped on the wine, momentarily in another world it seemed.

'Louise?' Henry squeezed her arm a little harder to gain her attention, 'Shall I send for the physician?'

Louise suddenly bent over and uttered a sob of pain, 'Henry, I think, I think, the midwife would be a wiser choice. I believe the baby is coming!'

It was a long, painful twenty-two hours before Louise finally gave birth to an apparently healthy boy. His cries soon filled the house. He fed and slept well…too well. Nothing seemed to disturb him. The crashing of a summer thunderstorm failed to awaken him. A raised voice failed to disturb him. However, he appeared normal in all other respects. Some three months later, when the scullery maid dropped a pail of water by his cradle and he didn't react, Louise wondered if his hearing was all it should be. The evidence of his deafness became clearer and more obvious as he grew. By the time he was one year old they knew for certain he could not hear. He was living in a comfortable soundless cocoon, unaware of any sounds, distraction and, of course, his worried parents' voices.

The servants were talking in the kitchen, when one remembered her mother saying that the house was once home to another with a similar condition. The cook, Penny, went back to see her elderly Mother who once worked as a server at *The Gentlemen's Rest*. 'You are right daughter, there was a lovely lady called Grace who lived there who was a mute, and if I remember she had a daughter who was almost totally deaf? What an unfortunate coincidence. I have heard others gossip that the house is not one in which children are born with all their senses intact. Poor boy, poor parents,' she said sympathetically.

Penny relayed the news back to the kitchen staff. Inevitably, the rumours reached Henry and his wife. They initially dismissed them. Upon further checking, Henry did indeed discover that previous babies born at the house had suffered from birth defects.

'Surely it must be a terrible coincidence?' asked a puzzled Louise. She found it hard to believe in such rumours, but then again, it seemed they might have some truth in them.

'It may well be my dear, but if we plan to have other children here, do you want to take that risk?' asked Henry in his most diplomatic voice. In this case he was happy to accede to his wife's demands, no matter how inconvenient they might be.

They agonised for weeks. Though both claimed not to be superstitious, it was a manifestation they could not ignore. They would never forgive themselves if their second child had a similar affliction. When Louise announced that she would never even consider *conceiving* in the house again, Henry hastily purchased a property in adjacent Guildhall Street. The Whyting street house would be rented.

Unfortunately, that would be the cause of yet more tribulations.

Chapter 19

~1645~

'I have proof she is a witch!'

Henry Jermyn inwardly groaned, the town was going witch finding mad, and he had the latest accuser standing in his study, claiming to have faced one outside the house in Whyting street where he was living as one of Henry's tenants.

'Pray calm down Mr Cooper, and explain to me why you believe a witch visited my house, causing you so much upset?'

'She came to the door selling chattels. Then told me that she could divine strange emanations from the house. She offered to come in and perform some cleansing ritual for two groats, which I declined and sent her on her way. When I opened the front door later, huge cobwebs with red spiders inside were festooned everywhere. 'Tis most upsetting sir, I demand you do something. She is obviously a witch.'

Henry's initial reaction was to dismiss the man's claim as part of the witch hysteria running unchecked throughout Bury. It all started when the self-styled "witch finder general" Matthew Hopkins set up a court to try a staggering 125 suspected witches and wizards from around the county. Men, women and children were dragged into his court, including an eighty-year-old vicar, John Lowes from Brandeston, who had already confessed his guilt.

The Witch Finder carried the long proven guide to identifying witches. Called *The Hammer of Witches*, the book was written centuries earlier by two monks. Reprinted several times it was the reference source for all things witchcraft, and he followed it to the letter.

The town was alive with stories of witches and their magic. Every household seemed to know somebody who might be one. Any strange occurrence or behaviour would be blamed on witchcraft. To deflect attention, many women would accuse friends or neighbours of being witches or in bed with the devil. Be warned if you were a single, old woman living with cats. Or practised any kind of healing, did not attend church, or worst of all, had a birthmark. You would be targeted by Matthew Hopkins and his band of rabid followers. No excuse was acceptable, no defence good enough to deflect him from finding the accused guilty, when more often than not, they weren't.

Henry was acutely aware of the dangers if he ignored his tenant's strident demands. As the property owner, he was responsible for the house; dismiss Mr Cooper's claims and he could find himself in the local gaol accused of owning a coven or something equally outrageous. Then again, to overreact might encourage Mr Cooper and the other tenants to start believing something *was* strange about the house.

He patiently listened to Mr Cooper's rantings then after a few minutes showed him out promising that he'd be round in due course to inspect the evidence.

Louise was seated in the main room, reading, when Henry came to find her. She looked up to see the concern on his face, 'What did that man want Henry? He seemed very agitated when he arrived.

'Indeed, he was my dearest. I would like to believe he is a touch zany. He is claiming someone visited our previous house and told him it was haunted in some way. Then covered the door in cobwebs after she left. Seems a little far-fetched to me, but I best go look for myself. Do you wish to come with me?'

Louise replied frostily, 'Absolutely not, I am with child and there is no way I am entering that house in my condition. You seem to have forgotten its unfortunate provenance concerning children and their afflictions? Henry, wild horses would not drag me there.'

Now it was Henry's turn to look incredulous, 'I thought we agreed those problems were just unfortunate coincidences? Are you saying you believe our house has some kind of curse upon it? I am disappointed in you Louise.'

Louise replied, barely containing her anger, 'You may be willing to risk our child's future Henry, but I am not. Indeed, I am thinking whether I ever want to go back and live in that house at all.'

'A subject for further discussion I believe,' said a chastised Henry. He shrugged his shoulders, collected his coat and left the house.

Henry turned into Whyting street and immediately saw his front door still festooned with huge cobwebs looking like heavy grey curtains. He brushed them aside with his walking stick, knocked on the door and entered the house.

Mr Cooper and his wife, Elaine, came scampering across the great hall like eager puppies, 'Did you see the cobwebs, sir? We left them there so you could observe them for yourself, and show we were not lying,' explained Mr Cooper, his voice rising in excitement, or was it fear?.

Henry acknowledged the obvious, 'Yes of course I saw them, hard to miss. I would ask you now to remove them, your point has been made. I would suggest in the current atmosphere pervading Bury, we both wish to avoid any suggestion of witchcraft in this house.'

Suddenly looking worried, Mr Cooper shouted at his wife, 'Our landlord makes a sound argument. Elaine get a brush and sweep them into the street, quickly woman!' Silently, she scurried off to do his bidding.

'What of the other tenants in the house, are they aware of this...event?' queried Henry.

'No sire, they are all out at the moment, thankfully. What do you think we should do now? We could ask a priest to come and bless the house?'

Henry tried a conciliatory approach, 'I understand your concerns Mr Cooper, however as I have just said, I think we would do well to let this matter rest for a few weeks until we investigate further. The town is a cauldron of witch hunting activities and accusations, I would not want to become involved, would you?'

Fear and reason wormed its way into Mr Cooper's mind, he nodded in agreement, 'Yes, yes, much as I would like to pursue our strange visitor's claims, perhaps it is best left for calmer times? Clearly she was trying to stir up trouble for us, probably does the same thing at every house she visits.'

'You could well be right Mr Cooper, let us take this no further for the moment. I am glad we are in agreement. If there is nothing further concerning you, I will now take my leave of you.'

It was dusk as he walked up Whyting street then turned into the alley leading to Guildhall Street. Henry was too wrapped up in his thoughts to see a woman lurking in a doorway. She moved quickly from the shadows to stand in front of him. Startled, he drew his dagger, then saw it was a woman as she pulled back the hood covering her face, 'God strewth woman, what do you want? You are lucky you do not have a dagger in your stomach.'

The woman was rake thin, gaunt with sunken, dull eyes. Her unkempt dirty grey hair obscured much of her face. Her clothing was ragged and filthy. Henry assumed she was a beggar. 'If you are intending to ask for money, I have none on me, so be on your way.'

In a croaking whisper, she leant closer to him and said, 'Sire, it is what I have for you that will be of concern. I am not after your money.'

Henry's interest was piqued long enough for him to stop and listen, 'And what might that be?' he demanded.

'I was at your house earlier. Sir, even without entering I knew all was not well there. It has an unhappy and corrupt miasma emanating from it....'

Henry cut her short, 'Madam, enough of your hocus pocus, there is nothing wrong with my house, now be off with you before I turn you into the authorities as a witch.'

The woman held his arm in a surprisingly strong grip, 'Sir, I know this sounds like witchcraft, and maybe that is the cause of the malevolence I felt. But would I be right in saying that children have been born, or have suffered strange defections, while living there?'

Momentarily stunned by the woman's accurate claim, he spluttered, 'Well, now that you say it, my daughter was born deaf and we have heard rumours of children who have lived there in the past suffering some...afflictions. How can you deduce this? You must be a witch!'

'You may call me what you will sir, but I have always been able to feel the presence of good and evil in a house. It is both a

199

curse and a blessing and it has caused me much pain over the years. Yet seldom have I been wrong. Your house is infected with a curse of some kind that affects the youngest souls. Somewhere a hex, of considerable strength resides there. I know not where, or how it can be reversed. I just know it is present.'

Henry listened with increasing disbelief, 'This is all gibberish you witch, if you are trying to extort money from me, you shall not succeed. I have never heard such nonsense. Be off with you!'

The women said no more, slinking off into the gloom of the early evening. Despite his bravado in dismissing her allegations, Henry felt disturbed. One cannot argue that some children born in the house had been malformed in some way, but because of some ancient curse? Really, Henry reasoned with himself, it's all too far-fetched to have any truth in it. Nevertheless, he decided to keep the conversation secret from Louise for fear of upsetting her while in such a delicate state.

Six months later, Henry and Louise welcomed their new baby, Katie. She was healthy and without any obvious maladies. Was this due to her being conceived and born away from the house in Whyting street, or just a happy coincidence? Notwithstanding the fortune Henry had spent on the house, he decided to soon sell it and tell no one of its unfortunate history.

Chapter 20

The morbid, fanatical fascination with witchcraft continued. All through July and August the witch finder trials continued. Of the 125 accused (some say it was closer to two hundred), Judges Edmund Calamy and John Godbolt found sixty guilty and sentenced them to hang. Others avoided punishment when the approach of the King's Army caused the trials to be halted allowing some to escape to their homes, many others remained in gaol. It was not a time to be associated in any way with witchcraft. A subtle insinuation, a chance remark associating you even tenuously with the subject would find you in gaol with every likelihood the only release being at the end of the hangman's noose.

It was early in July, Henry was in the Court building meeting another lawyer to discuss their respective client's lawsuit, where one was suing the other for a property sale that had gone wrong.

There was a commotion as a phalanx of guards and soldiers herded in a group of accused witches. They were the latest in a long line of, mainly women, who were sent for trial in front of the hated and feared 'Witchfinder General', Matthew Hopkins.

Henry turned to his fellow lawyer, Dominic Hooper, 'It always seems to be poor young women of little standing that end up in these courts, I wonder why?'

Dominic leant closer to Henry so as not to be overheard, 'Judge Hopkins follows with religious zeal, the tenets in the *Hammer of Witches* book. I have read some of it, and it claims women are more impressionable than men, have greater...er... sexual appetites, so their lust leads them to accept even the Devil as a lover. I cannot remember all the tell tale signs, but these are some. He may well ask some of them to take tests which prove they are witches or not.'

Henry looked at him in disbelief, 'Tests? What are these tests?'

'Well, in truth, Henry, they are tests none of them ever seem to pass. I know one is to read out loud the Lord's prayer, if they falter or cannot remember it, that is one sign they are a witch. They will have been searched for witches' marks on their body that feel no pain when pricked with needles, that is another test. Of course the most familiar one is to be thrown into the River Lark at its deepest point. If they float they are a witch, if they sink, they are not. But then it is often too late to save them,' he finished his explanation with a sorry shake of his head.

In amongst the gaggle of frightened women was an elderly man. He looked confused and disorientated, as though searching in the crowd of onlookers for a friend or some assistance.

'God strewth!' exclaimed Henry, 'What is that poor old man doing here? I think I recognise him. Yes, he's a vicar, I heard him preach once. Boring but made some excellent points if I remember. How on earth has he ended up here? Do you know his name perchance?'

'I don't, let me ask one of the guards.' Minutes later, fighting his way back through the noisy crowd, he informed Henry the man was called John Lowes from the village of Brandeston.

Henry was appalled. He knew only too well the danger in defending an accused witch, but his conscience couldn't allow this unfortunate old man to meet his accusers without some form of legal defence. 'I must find out if I can do anything to help that vicar, this is too outrageous for even maniacs like Hopkins to send him to the gallows.'

'Henry, please don't do this,' pleaded Dominic. 'Your reputation will be tarnished or even ruined, if you defend a witch. Nothing good can come of this grand gesture. I urge you to let justice take its course!'

Henry turned angrily, 'That is exactly the point sir, this is not justice, it is a one man crusade that is putting innocent people to death. I cannot help them all, but I intend to try and help this poor man.'

With those parting words, Henry elbowed his way into the court and waited for the trial to begin. With eighteen people accused, most of whom had already pleaded guilty. Hopkins and his fellow judge Edmund Calamy handed down the death sentence in rapid succession to each one. Before doing so, they cursorily asked if the accused had anything to say in their defence. Few said anything, it was all too late. John Lowes was the last to stand before the judges. He stood up and looked at the two men who held his fate in their hands, and in a remarkably steady and clear voice now proclaimed his innocence.

The two judges looked up, surprised, but indifferent. Calamy resembled a bird of prey, thought Henry. His skin stretched tightly across his face, a large hooked nose with a tight small mouth and perpetually mean, expressionless eyes. He was a quiet person who displayed no feelings, showed no mercy. By contrast, Judge Hopkins radiated authority and an absolute belief in his position of power. A rotund man with eyes almost hidden behind his fleshy jowls, he looked benign until he launched into one of his raving anti-witch outbursts. Liberally quoting from the *Hammer of Witches,* unfailingly following its advice and guidance, he brooked no argument.

Calamy was dismissive, 'It is too late for a change of heart, you purveyor of magic, you have pleaded guilty and many have seen the results of your communications with the Devil....there is no defence to your evil..'

The vicar looked confused. He stuttered a brief response, "My Lords, whatever confession I made was forced from my lips... by the brute force of the guards. They starved me, allowed me no sleep and beat me each day. These men are barbarians... I succumbed to their threats and brutality and admitted guilt to something I would never have done. I...I am a man of the cloth, and have been for forty five years. As God is my witness, I have committed no evil. I..I implore mercy from...my Lords.'

Henry chose this moment to stand up in front of the two judges and announce to the whole court's consternation that he was representing the Vicar against charges of witchcraft.

204

The two judges said nothing for a moment, then rounded angrily on Henry. Judge Hopkins, seething, demanded Henry be silent, 'It is too late for you to intercede on behalf of this wizard, he has already admitted his guilt.'

Suddenly finding his voice again, the Vicar shouted across the courtroom, 'I was tortured and threatened to extract my guilty plea. By the grace of God and in the eyes of the Lord, I am innocent!'

'Hush man, keep your silence!' bellowed Judge Calamy.

Before he could continue, Henry interrupted, 'My Lords, justice must be seen to be done, even for a wizard. Especially for a man of the cloth who has had no accusations laid against him in all the years of looking after his parishioners. He has led a blameless and holy life.'

The judges, unused to having someone argue so articulately against them, hesitated for a moment. They also sensed the mood in the court turning against them, there were murmurs of agreement with Henry's words.

'We cannot waste more time. Unless you can think of a quick way to prove this man's innocence, he will hang like the rest of them before the day's end,' said Judge Hopkins.

Remembering the information Dominic had previously given him, Henry had an idea. 'My Lords, one of the definitive signs of a witch or wizard is that they cannot recite, or remember, verses from the scriptures, or even the Lord's Prayer. If Vicar Lowes can pass this test, I ask that the accusations against him be dismissed.'

A few shouts of agreement came from the crowd, now fascinated by the legal duel being fought out in front of them.

The two judges briefly conferred, then with a curt, 'So be it,' Judge Calamy acceded to Henry's challenge.

Henry turned to the bemused Vicar, asking, 'Do you understand what you have to do sir, if you can recite the Lord's Prayer without error you are a free man!'

The vicar nodded his head, 'Yes sire, I do.' Now realising his life depended on his memory working properly, he composed himself and started, 'Our Father who art in Heaven....'

'Oh that is far too easy for a Vicar,' interrupted Judge Hopkins. 'Let me choose a verse from the scriptures for him to repeat. Let me see now,' he pulled a copy of the Bible that was always on the judge's bench. He flicked through, then with a smirk on his face demanded of the Vicar, 'Recite Deuteronomy 18:9–12.'

For a moment, the whole court sat silent, it was a pernicious test, few would be able to pass. The Vicar stared straight ahead directly at Judge Hopkins, then said, 'With pleasure my Lords, I believe it says:

When you enter the land the Lord your God is giving you, do not learn to imitate the detestable ways of the nations there. Let no one be found among you who sacrifices their son or daughter in the fire, who practices divination or sorcery, interprets omens, engages in witchcraft, or casts spells, or who is a medium or spiritist or who consults the dead. Anyone who does these things is detestable to the Lord.'

Judge Hopkins looked up from the Bible, furious he'd been outfoxed, but knowing he now had no choice but to declare the Vicar innocent. He snarled, 'You have proved your point Vicar, now leave my courtroom before I find another charge to bring against you.'

The whole courtroom erupted into cheers as the elderly Vicar smiled at his victory over the tyranny of two bloodthirsty judges.

He stood still for a minute until the noise had died down then with newly found confidence said, 'If I may, my Lords? Perhaps you may like to look up *Isaiah 10:1-3*, it is particularly appropriate for what has happened here today.'

With that, he left the courtroom, and walked over to Henry. They shook hands and the Vicar indicated they should talk away from the crowd. Outside the courthouse, he pulled Henry to one side, 'I cannot thank you enough sir for your help in saving my life today. Why did you speak up for me? Have we met before?"

Henry smiled, 'No Vicar, we have not. Though I have heard you preach. I was just in the right place at the right time. I am a lawyer and could not bear to see a man of the cloth accused of such a crime without putting up a fight. Those two judges are zealots who care nothing for the law. Anyone who is paid based on how many people they convict cannot be fair. I was determined to see justice done today. I only wish I could have helped the others. But I knew you alone could pass one of the tests for not being a witch and you repaid my faith in you.'

The Vicar smiled, his lined face suddenly lighting up, reflecting the relief he felt at avoiding an appointment with the executioner, 'Well, I thank you sir for your faith in me, and for your well-timed intervention. I will say a prayer for you tonight when I return to my church.'

The two men shook hands and went their separate ways. As he left the courthouse heading towards Westgate street and home, he knew only too well, the Vicar's prayers would do little to combat the wrath of the two Judges he had just humiliated. He feared their retribution would be brutal, if he faced them again.

When he arrived home, Henry went to his study and picked up the Bible. He was intrigued to find out what the Psalm said the Vicar had suggested the judges read. He found it and smiled:

Woe to those who enact evil statutes
And to those who constantly record unjust decisions,
So as to deprive the needy of justice
And rob the poor of My people of their rights,
So that widows may be their spoil
And that they may plunder the orphans.
Now what will you do in the day of punishment,
And in the devastation which will come from afar?
To whom will you flee for help?
And where will you leave your wealth?

Chapter 21

~1649~

I n 1649, the victorious Parliamentarians sentenced Charles I to death. His execution resulted in the only period of Republican rule in British history, during which military leader Oliver Cromwell ruled as Lord Protector of the Commonwealth. This period is known as the Interregnum, and lasted for eleven years until 1660 when Charles's son, Charles II, was restored to the throne.

'King Charles is Dead. Long live the Republic!'

Standing on the steps of the Corn Exchange, the town crier bellowed the latest news to an astonished crowd. King Charles 1st had been beheaded. The Royalists lost the civil war to the Roundheads led by Oliver Cromwell. The country was now run by a Parliament. England was a Republic! The Monarchy, the House of Lords, and incredibly the Anglican Church, were abolished. And Christmas would no longer be a holiday!

William Bernstein stood with his wife, Maria, listening to the list of changes to be imposed by what was left of the Parliament.

Despondently he whispered, 'Instead of a profligate King we have a band of buffoons now running the country. No doubt the Puritans will make hay, and our lives a misery....'

'Ssh, William, please, keep your voice down, such talk will get you into trouble. We will just have to make the best of it. Let us go home to supper and discuss in private how to keep our business going in these difficult times.'

They left the crowd listening to the litany of new demands and laws and wandered around the market. The town crier deliberately planned his announcement to be heard on the busiest day of the week. People came from miles around to sell their wares at the biggest market in the county. It was the main source of fresh meat, fish and vegetables for the townsfolk.

As they walked, Maria had to raise her voice to make herself heard over the stallholders shouting their wares, the plaintive cries of dozens of caged animals and birds awaiting their fate and the cacophony of the hundreds of people milling around, chatting while they shopped. The shops around the sides of the market square had opened their large windows and were selling everything a household could need—or a person could eat.

'Let's buy a pie, I am hungry, and some ale to wash it down,' suggested Maria.

William did her bidding, walked over to a bakers shop, and bought two huge beef pies, still warm from the oven. They stopped at another seller to get some ale to wash them down. The choice of vendors selling ready cooked food was enormous as most people did not have the time, or space, to cook at home.

For an hour they walked, taking in the noise, sights and smells, a heady mixture for every sense. The aromas drifting through the market stretched from mouthwatering food to retch-inducing sewage and animal dung. The market was in its fourth century of existence, more than ever the beating heart of this prosperous market town. As they turned into Abbeygate street from the Buttermarket, the crowd of shoppers was packed solid, making for slow progress. William became separated from Maria in the crush.

Suddenly, she felt a sharp tug on her purse, instinctively Maria pulled back, turning to see who was trying to take it from her. She looked behind, a young boy, probably no more than ten years old, was pulling hard to dislodge it from her shoulder.

She lashed out in anger, screaming, 'Stop, stop you, you scoundrel. Thief! Thief!' Maria kept shouting, hoping she would be heard by William, or someone would come to her aid.

Hearing his wife's cries, William turned round and wrestled his way through the crowd towards her. He saw her stagger backwards as the strap was cut. He caught sight of a small boy clutching her purse, practically crawling along the ground as he made his escape. It was all over within seconds. By the time he reached his distraught wife, the boy was lost in the melee. He held her, she was shaking in fear and frustration, 'Did you see where he went…the boy?' she asked, frantically looking around.

'It's too late Maria, in this crush we will never find him,' replied William. 'More importantly, are you hurt?'

'No, no, I'm fine, just a little shaken. I am ashamed I didn't put up stronger resistance to the little thief. He will be happy with his haul, there were several crowns in there, plus my favourite gold bracelet I had put in there for safe keeping!'

'The money is not important, we should be grateful you suffered no physical harm. Come let us make our way home. You must lie down for a while to recover from the shock.'

She linked her arm in his for support and walked down Whyting street towards their recently purchased home. Not for the first time, Maria couldn't understand why a wealthy lawyer like Henry Jermyn would sell it so cheaply. However, they were happy in the new spacious home which they'd furnished with care and at great expense. Their two grown children loved being in the town rather than at their farm in Cavenham. They left the eldest boy, Matthew, to run the farm when they moved into Bury. So far, he had done an admiral job, allowing them to concentrate on their other business as money lenders.

'This is now a street of splendid houses, don't you think? Thankfully the workhouse has moved to Moyses Hall to be part of the town's gaol, it helps improve the value of properties I would presume?' Receiving no response, she gently dug William in the ribs, 'Husband, do you not hear me? What is on your mind that makes you deaf to my conversation?'

'Sorry my love. But this incident has set me thinking. We have a lot of money, gold and silver plate at the house. Maybe we are being too trusting, as money lenders we are targets for theft and assault. Perhaps we should make our house more secure?'

'You worry too much, my love. That cutpurse was an isolated incident. I am annoyed and upset, but let us not assume we are living amongst a den of thieves. Our bigger problem I believe is how to invest our money wisely and for a greater profit than in the past. We are facing uncertain times without a King or proper government. We must think carefully and with prudence where we place our money.'

William looked admiringly at his wife, 'As ever Maria, you speak wisely. Let us have a quiet supper this evening and discuss these matters.'

When they arrived at the front door Maria stopped, a worried look on her face, 'Oh heavens! My purse contained the keys to the house. That rascal now has them.' She looked up and down the street, 'If he has followed us, he will know where we live, can you see him anywhere, William?'

'Now 'tis you who worry too much,' William chastised her. 'He will be too busy spending your crowns and pawning the bracelet to think about following us. If it eases your concerns I will get the locksmith to come and replace the locks. Firstly, we need to get into our own house! I shall try and gain entry via our neighbour's garden, into our backyard. Wait here.'

Peering cautiously round the corner of Whyting and Churchgate street, the young cutpurse, Davy, and his elder brother watched the couple stop outside their house, then the husband disappeared into their neighbour's garden. Minutes later the front door opened and the woman went inside. Seeing where they lived, Dan exclaimed, 'Strewth! My uncle used to live there. What was his name...yes, Henry...Henry...Jermyn! Only went

213

there the once. Bit of a stuck up lawyer. Bet there's plenty of valuables in there, if those people can afford a big house like that.'

He stopped talking and thought for a moment, 'Look, we only have a short time to take advantage of having their keys. They will change the locks soon for sure. Let us come back tonight and reap the rewards of your efforts. You did well, Davy. We shall finally eat well.'

It was almost totally dark when the two brothers returned close to midnight. What sliver of light the moon provided was diluted by the jettied upper storeys of the houses on either side leaning over the street. They had brought one small candle and tinder box to help find their way around the house. Dan gently inserted the key into the lock, it turned easily and quietly. The heavy oak door opened with the slightest of squeaks, which in the silence seemed loud enough to wake the entire household. The boys stood stock still, waiting to see if anyone stirred. Nothing moved.

They closed the door, lit the candle and found their way to the great hall. Along one wall was a huge dresser with plates, goblets, jugs and other household valuables. Dan picked one up and weighed it in his hand, 'Strewth, I think these are silver, brother. There's a fortune here. Put as many as you can in the sack while I go and look around—be quiet about it!'

'Don't leave me Dan!' pleaded the young boy. Not willing to admit he was petrified of the dark—and fearing discovery if they spent more than a few minutes in the house.

'Oh! Don't be a milksop. Here take this candle,' he lit and handed his brother a candlestick from the dresser.

'I'll be back in a minute, work quickly.'

Dan and the tiny amount of light thrown by his candle barely illuminated the farther reaches of the great hall as he looked around for more easy to carry swag. He guessed the money was in a safe box in the owner's bedroom, a tantalising thought, but too risky. He hadn't stayed out of gaol all his years as a thief and house breaker by being greedy, or stupid.

He padded quietly around the large room and picked up some weighty candlesticks. A quick look underneath revealed assay marks confirming their high silver content. He tucked them under his arm and continued his search. His heart almost stopped when he heard a door open and footsteps coming from the owners' rooms somewhere upstairs. He scampered across to his brother, and whispered, 'Quick! Get out of here, someone's coming downstairs.'

The young boy was still gently lowering plates into the already bulging sack. Acting on his brother's urgent command, he tried to pick it up and sling it over his shoulder. He grunted in surprise at how heavy it was and promptly dropped it to the ground, a muffled crash followed.

A disembodied voice from the top of the stairs shouted into the great hall's darkness, 'Who is there? I am armed with a pistol and will not hesitate to use it!'

'Shit Dan, let's go, fuck the sack, I'm not getting shot for some silver plates.' With that Davy bolted out of the great hall, down the hallway and into the street, his elder brother, seconds behind him clutching three candlesticks, 'Run brother, run,' urged Dan, pushing the small boy in the back to get him moving.

Ten minutes later, now sure no one was following, they stopped running to catch their breath. Elated and relieved, Dan slapped his brother on the shoulder, 'Shit Davy that was close!' After a moment's pause he asked, 'Why'd you drop the sack? That had a fortune in it, enough to get us on a ship to America you dolthead.'

The young boy fired back, 'You're the dolthead Dan. We should have just taken what we could carry and then skedaddled. Not go searching the house for more stuff. We could be shot dead by now. Or hanged if we were caught.'

Dan cuffed the young boy round the back of the head, 'You stupid dunderhead, don't answer me back, next time do as I tell you, and we'll be rich.' He pushed his young brother roughly in the back and they headed home towards their room in a house on Southgate street. Dan was annoyed they had let slip so many valuable items, but at least they still had some silver candlesticks to fence at the recently opened pawn shop in the Buttermarket.

Two days later, they looked up at the three large balls hanging from a bracket above a shop door. 'This is it Davy, let's see what money we can get for these candlesticks. We'll bring the bracelet you got off that lady back another day. Don't want to get 'im suspicious.' They walked in and looked around. On the walls and the floor were hundreds of household and farming items people had brought in to exchange for cash. If they didn't pay the money back within thirty days, the pawnbroker could sell them.

Putting on a show of bravado, Dan walked up to the man behind the counter.

'Morning sir, we found these in the river when we were fishing, what can you give us for them?'

Barely containing his suspicions, the pawnbroker took the beautifully made silver candlesticks. Looking at the assay marks, he saw they were made in London by a well known silversmith twenty years ago.

'Found them in the river eh? Wondered who'd throw these valuable pieces away? They are worth a tidy sum.'

Feigning innocence, Dan replied, 'Don't know sir, case of their bad luck is our good fortune.'

'Indeed young man. Indeed. Look, I cannot value these myself, let me go and find the owner and he can come back and make you a much better offer than I. Can you stay a few minutes?'

Without waiting for a reply, the man went into the back of the shop to find his son, 'Brian, hurry to the court offices, I believe we have a couple of cutpurses here trying to fence some stolen silverware. Get the constable or a guard to come back here as quickly as possible. I will try and detain them.' His son scurried out of the back door into Skinner street and ran to the courthouse.

The pawnbroker waited for a few minutes then went back to try and keep the two young men, now looking increasingly nervous, from leaving the premises.

'Sorry to keep you waiting, it seems the owner is in the alehouse. My son has gone to fetch him. He will be back presently.' All three of them stood in an awkward silence for some minutes.

Then Dan's sixth sense, one that had got him out of many a tight corner in the past, prodded him to take action, 'Thank you sir, we'll come back later. Brother, let us go and get some breakfast.' Ignoring the pawnbroker's protestations to wait, the two boys hastily turned to leave the pawnshop. It was too late. They opened the door to be confronted by two burly men, both carrying pistols. Before they could utter a word both were being frog marched off to the gaol.

'Dan, I'm scared, what's gonna happen to us?' The young boy huddled next to his big brother. They were in the cells at Moyses Hall, and had been for several hours after being roughly thrown in there following their arrest.

Dan tried to sound upbeat, 'Don't know brother. Have to wait and see. Maybe they'll just put us in the pillory, they can't prove we stole those candlesticks.' They didn't have long to wait to find out their fate.

Justice was dispensed quickly at the Bury Assizes. A day later, they were dragged up before an elderly grizzled looking judge, who stared at them through rheumy, compassionless eyes. His severe look indicated he would show no mercy towards the two young men, brought before him. He had seen too many cut purses to feel any sympathy, or show any sympathy. Without looking up, he fired off a series of questions:

'Names? And Ages?'

'My name is Dan, sir. I am fifteen, this is my brother, Davy, he's eight, sir.'

'Where are your parents?'

'Don't know sir…long since gone.'

'Anyone who can vouch for why you might have those valuable items in your possession?'

They both fell silent. Then with a sudden flash of inspiration, Dan blurted out, 'Yessir, my uncle, Henry Jermyn.'

The judge looked up quizzically at Dan, 'You are related to lawyer Jermyn?'

'Indeed we are sir, a fine uncle he is too. I am sure he would vouch for our good character if given the chance, sir.'

Skeptically, the judge looked down at the two scruffy, dirty waifs, 'I find that hard to believe, but we shall send for him. I should warn you boy, if you are lying or wasting my time, it will only make matters worse for you. A lot worse.'

Dan and Davy nodded mutely. They were taken back to the cells to wait and see if their last chance at avoiding a painful punishment would work.

Henry was working in his study when a messenger came from the court with news that his two nephews were in trouble and needed his help. He took the note, found Louise with the baby in the front parlour, and asked, 'Do you remember anything about some relatives called Dan and Davy? They claim I am related to them? The name Dan does stick in my mind.'

Louise thought for a moment, 'Weren't they your half sister's boys? We lost touch with them after she died a few years ago.'

'Yes, yes, of course, I only met the older one, Dan. Bit of a wild child from what I can remember. Well I have just received a message, it seems they are in gaol accused of theft. They want me to come and vouch for them. Dammit and I have so much work, I really cannot afford such petty diversions.'

'I understand, husband, but I think you owe it to your deceased half sister to go and see if you can help. It will only take an hour or two. I remember when she died you expressed some regret you had not kept in touch with her. She had been deserted by her husband, and I think was living in a poor house in Woolpit working as a spinner. It can do no harm to go and see those boys. They may be innocent after all. Go on, be a good uncle!'

Gruffly Henry agreed, 'Your words have rightly pricked my conscience into doing the proper thing. However, I believe it will be a waste of my time.' He grabbed his coat and cursing under his breath at the inconvenience of it all, strode quickly to the Moyses Hall gaol.

'My God, how can you keep people in this filth?' Henry asked the guard as he took him to one of the underground cells. The place was damp, dark and stank of human waste. Henry held a kerchief to his nose to try and blot out the stink.

The guard concurred, 'I agree sir, but it's all the town can afford so I'm told. Most aren't here for long, if you know what I mean.' He stopped by a cell, 'These are the two cutpurses you wanted to see.''

The guard opened the door and Henry's senses were assailed by even stronger disgusting smells, 'Please God, where can I take them so the odour is not so repulsive?'
The guard was obdurate, 'I'm afraid I cannot allow that sir, they would probably make a run for it. More than my job is worth. My apologies, sir.'

Henry dismissed him, annoyed at his unhelpful attitude. He looked at the two young urchins sitting on the floor. They looked frightened, in need of a good meal and wash. Pathetic sights the both of them, thought Henry. The elder boy stood up and offered his hand.

Reluctantly Henry shook it, 'Sir, Uncle, we thank you for coming to see us, you are our last chance to avoid punishment. My name is Dan, this is my brother Davy. I met you a long time ago when my mother visited your house. Do you remember, sir?'

'Yes, yes I do, your mother was my half sister. Now what have you done and how do you think I can help you?'

Relieved that his Uncle was willing to help, Dan explained. 'We have been accused of stealing some candlesticks and trying to pawn them. We was in desperate need of food. It was the only thing I could think to do. Do you think you can help us? Our Mother always spoke highly and with great fondness of you sir.'

Henry doubted that was the case at all. Nevertheless he was here now, he may as well see if he could help. 'So, you did steal them? You can tell me, I am not obliged to reveal our conversation to anyone else.'

Davy, tears in his eyes, admitted so, 'Yessir, we did.'

'Where from?' asked Henry.
'The people who now live in your old house in Whyting street.'

'William and Maria? Oh God's teeth, why did you choose that house?' Henry was horrified they'd robbed friends of his.

Dan looked at Davy, who shrugged his shoulders, in a "you may as well tell him" gesture. So Dan retold the story of stealing the lady's purse, the keys they found in it. Following the owners home, later breaking in and escaping with the candlesticks. Henry listened, appalled at the boy's larceny, their gall at breaking into his old house. And the final stupidity of trying to pawn the stolen goods.

Henry told them, 'You know you could hang for this, don't you?'

They knew they were in big trouble, but not severe enough to face a death sentence. Davy burst into tears hugging his brother for support. Dan looked shocked, the blood drained from his face, leaving him pale and stunned with fear.

'That cannot be so sir, they were but candlesticks?'

'Dan,' Henry explained, 'if the items are worth more than one pound, it can mean a death sentence. Together with the bracelet and the coins you stole, your crime exceeds that.'

'There must be a way, surely sir. Tis the first time we are before the judge. Will he not show mercy?' Panic rose in Dan's voice as the seriousness of their position dawned on him.

'Thieving is taken very seriously in this town, there is a lot of it happening. The judge wants to set examples to dissuade others from committing such crimes.'

Henry thought for a minute, 'Do you still have the bracelet and coins?'

'We have the bracelet, we used some of the money for food sir. There are still two crowns left,' replied Dan. 'Why do you ask, sir?'

The germ of an idea was brewing in Henry's mind. He told the boys he would be back the following day.

His first stop was to visit his old house and see William and Maria. He explained the two miscreants were distant relatives. That they had been abandoned by their parents at an early age and were now living on their wits, occasionally resorting to crime to feed themselves. That he would get their candlesticks, bracelet and all of their money back. (He would make up the shortfall himself.) Under these circumstances, he asked, would they consider asking the judge to be lenient on the boys? Henry's imploring speech persuaded them to agree. The thought of an eight-year-old boy being hanged over three candlesticks would not sit easy on their conscience.

Next stop was the curmudgeonly Judge Stewart, who Henry knew from countless court cases. He was a tough, old fashioned judge who believed the punishment should be equal to twice the crime. He listened impassively to Henry's proposal. The fact the victims were prepared to forgive the boys, swayed him some way towards leniency. It was Henry's generous offer (prompted by Louise) to put the boys through school, and guarantee of no further misdemeanours, that persuaded him a day in the pillories and ten lashes would be sufficient punishment.

Dan and Davy, while mightily relieved they had escaped hanging, were still dreading their day in the pillory and the lashing—all done in public to cause maximum humiliation. There were four pillories set up in the market square. They were joined by two other men, both guilty of public drunkenness. It was a market day, the guards told them with glee, so expect a good sized audience to see their bare backsides. Adding maliciously, 'and a plentiful supply of stale and foul items to throw at you'

Two days later the boys were manhandled into the pillories. Davy because of his age was too small to reach the holes to secure his hands and head, until a guard helpfully found a box for him to stand on. Their trousers were soon by their ankles and the guards delivered ten thwacking blows with a four foot long birch stick to each of them. Davy tried not to cry but after the third stinging blow landed he blubbered uncontrollable, much to the mirth of the jeering crowd. Dan grimaced each time the stick landed on him, but held back the tears.

Then followed hours of insults from a raucous crowd enjoying seeing the four prisoners being pelted with anything rotten, dead or evil smelling. It was a source of amusement and entertainment for the crowd. By mid-afternoon, their humiliation came to a merciful end. The four criminals were released and hurried sheepishly off the pillories. One of Henry's servants was there to bring them back to his house. A bath was followed by their wounds being dressed by a female housemaid (painful and embarrassing) then a meal and a long lecture from Louise on the house rules while they were staying with them. Finally, Henry announced they would start school the following week.

It was a dramatic turn of events for the once destitute boys. In one week going from living by their wits on the streets, arrested, nearly being hung, a day in the pillories, to a safe, comfortable house and a secure future.

Henry and Louise's decision to take in Dan and Davy proved a wise and compassionate one. Both boys flourished under the stern eyes of their new foster parents and a solid education at the re-established Grammar School on Eastgate street.

From the proceeds of the Whyting street house, Henry invested the money supporting ventures in the new colony of America. Five years later, Dan would leave for Virginia to help run a tobacco plantation Henry had bought. His street smart acumen, combined with the newly acquired ability to read, write and understand maths, ensured him a wealthy future managing Henry's investments.

Dan never returned to England, his younger brother joined him in 1660. When Henry sold the plantation in 1666, they both moved to New York to take advantage of England's takeover of the city from the Dutch, and its subsequent expansion into one of North America's largest trading centres. They both became model citizens, wealthy, and forever in debt to their generous uncle.

Chapter 22

~1653~

After the upsetting break-in at the house, William and Maria sold up. It was the excuse they used to explain their decision to friends and relatives. In truth, their money lending venture suffered under the uncertainty of the Republic with many people defaulting on their loans. They moved to a smaller house in Hatter street.

The house lay empty for two years after it had been purchased by someone who wished his ownership to be kept a secret. Rumours claimed it was owned by Thomas Cullum, a wealthy London business man with pro-Royalist leanings. Whoever it was, he never took up residence himself.

Occasionally, men would come and stay for a few days, then leave, normally at night. The neighbours grew concerned as the building again began to show signs of neglect. After a particularly strong gale, the chimney was damaged sending bricks and mortar cascading into the street.

It took months before workmen arrived to rebuild it and repair the roof. The minimum was done to keep the house from decaying further.

The windows were permanently covered with shutters. The once carefully whitewashed walls lost their pristine finish and soon the wattle and daub underneath was exposed to the elements, further hastening its derelict appearance. Every time Henry walked by, he was upset to see the poor state of the house he once owned and treasured. From being one of the largest and best kept houses in Whyting Street, it was fast becoming an eyesore.

Inside, the house was in equally desolate condition, not that the occasional visitors seem to mind. They stayed only for a few days then moved on. Every few months, men from outside of the town, under strict instructions to talk to no one, came and gave the house a perfunctory clean, checked it was in good condition and carried out any urgent repairs. There was little furniture in the house. All the beautiful wall hangings, rugs and anything of value had been removed soon after its sale to the mysterious new owner.

Chapter 23 (1654)

'Can you see how many of the Royalist scum are in there?' asked Roger Courcy, leader of a small group of Roundhead soldiers watching the house in Whyting street. They were hiding across the street spying on people coming and going from the supposed Royalist meeting house. Informants had told them a meeting of the *Sealed Knot* was taking place.

The *Sealed Knot* was a secret army of men, loyal to the exiled King Charles II. There were many around the country in a loose federation with little central control. Formed with the King's blessing and, in theory, run by Sir Edward Blythe, they were in a hurry to usurp the Protectorate, mount a rebellion against Cromwell and assassinate him at the same time.

However, their ranks had been infiltrated by Cromwell's spy chief, John Thurloe. Hence the reason the house was under surveillance.

'I've counted six so far,' replied Kevin Browne, a particularly zealous member of the pro-Cromwell group. He fought in several battles against the King's forces and was ready to kill some more given the chance. He hated the Royalists, their taxes had reduced him to penury, the final insult when his anti-Cromwell master threw him out of his rented cottage, unwilling to accept his strident anti-Royalist opinions. 'I say we go in and kill them all, they are treasonous rats.' Kevin was bored and wanted some action to relieve the monotony and his desire for revenge.

'Yes they are, but we number only four, I would hesitate to enter their house until we know more of who is inside. Major General Haynes asked us only to collect information. He is not inclined to harm any local Royalists. Just throw them in gaol.' Roger was well aware of Kevin's hot headed hatred for any one of a Royalist persuasion. Keeping his bloodlust under control was proving tiresome. The other two men in the group were less enthusiastic in their beliefs and easier to manage.

They had been watching the large house for several hours and so far recognized no one who had entered. Just because it was owned by a known "King lover" as Kevin described them, did not mean everyone there was of a like mind, reasoned Roger.

Roger was following the orders of the group's commander, Hezekiah Haynes, who reported to George Fleetwood, the newly appointed Roundhead Major General for East Anglia. Hezekiah was a businessman, not a soldier, who did not want blood on his hands. He had specifically told Roger to watch and report back if he saw any known Royalist visiting the house. Not to start any trouble or violence.

Dusk was falling, there had been little recent activity in terms of visitors coming to the house. Once darkness fell, even seeing across the street would be difficult, let alone identifying anyone leaving or arriving. Relieved that he had contained Kevin's desire for action, and in truth, seen very little of interest to report back, Roger ordered his men to gather their belongings and make ready to leave.

He took one last look across the street and to his surprise saw two women holding hands leaving the house. Roger had not heard the front door open, or close and strangely they seemed to be talking to one another, but he could hear no words or sound as they walked up the street towards the town centre. Their dresses seemed a little old fashioned and one carried some kind of tablet in her hand. A shiver ran down Roger's back. He had not seen two women enter the house all day. Where had they come from?

He quickly called Kevin to the window, 'Look at those two women up the street, do you recognise them?'

Kevin looked out of the window. Bemused, he turned to Roger and said, 'Have you been drinking? The street is deserted, there's no one there. You're imagining things! If we can't kill those bastards in the house, let's go home.'

'But...but, I saw two women leave...I...I swear to it!' stammered Roger indignantly.

Kevin looked at him, disbelief in his voice, 'Sure you did. They say that house is haunted or cursed, reckon you saw a ghost. Or maybe you've been day dreaming! We've all had enough of this wasted day. Let's go home.'

As he turned from the window, it exploded into a meteor shower of shattered glass, simultaneously a musket ball drilled through Kevin's head drenching Roger in blood, brain and bone. For a second, he stood transfixed to the spot, unable to react. A second shot quickly followed the first, smashing into the wall behind him. He threw himself to the floor and crawled over to the two other men, now cowering in the corner of the room.

'Jesus and Mary, they have muskets. They will kill us all without coming close enough for us to fight back. Our swords and daggers are no match for their weapons. We must leave here, now,' ordered Roger.

One of the men pointed a shaking finger at Kevin's almost headless body, 'What shall we do with him?'

'Leave him, nothing we can do for him now. We can return later. Now let us leave here at once. Hurry for God's sake.'

The three shaken men hurriedly made their way downstairs out into College Walk. It was now almost dark. Before they could make haste their escape, two more musket shots cracked against the wall beside them. Brick and mortar shards exploded by their heads. The shots missed them by inches. Suddenly, out of the gloom rushed four men wielding guns and swords.

'Halt or we shoot again!' commanded one of the men. Roger and his two companions raised their hands and backed up to the wall, as if doing so would somehow offer protection.

'Wise move you Protestant traitors. Come with us at once. This way, and don't think about running, we will blast you to Hell if you try,' A tall man with a kerchief covering his face brandishing a musket, pointed the barrel back towards the house in Whyting street. The other three attackers surrounded Roger and his men, and poking them painfully in the back with their swords, urged them to move quickly.

Scared and bewildered by the sudden, frightening, turn of events the men did as instructed without putting up any resistance. Within minutes, they were manhandled into the house and downstairs to the cellar.

They were manacled and left in pitch darkness by their captors.

'What's going to happen to us, Roger?' asked a scared unseen voice from across the pitch dark cellar.

Roger could offer no comforting words, 'William? I do not know. I fear it won't be pleasant. These Royalists are thugs and killers, we must be brave and resist their threats for as long as we can. Reveal nothing about what we do or who works with us.'

The three men sat in petrified silence for what seemed like hours, each deep in his own thoughts as to how he might withstand the pain and torture likely to be inflicted upon him. Then they heard the sounds of boots clumping hurriedly across the floorboards above their heads. The trapdoor to the cellar was flung open and one of the captors ordered, 'Whoever is your leader, make themselves known.'

Roger looked up and meekly answered, 'It is I, Roger Whitworth of Risby.'

'Alright Roger of Risby, it's your lucky day, get up here.' The guard ordered him to climb up the steps. Legs weak with fear, Roger did as requested, stumbling at the top step, his balance off kilter with his hands tied behind him. Two men roughly grabbed him and pushed him into the great hall where a fire was burning, lighting up the dim room with long shadows. Sat on a chair warming herself was a woman. She motioned Roger to sit in the chair opposite. Roger tried to quell his fear, and his surprise, at seeing a woman in these strange circumstances.

He could not recognize her as she had a veil over her face. She spoke in a cultured accent and was dressed plainly, but in good quality clothing. Her hands showed no sign of having experienced any hard, physical labour. Roger guessed she was from an aristocratic family, attempting to look as someone from a lower class. She paused before saying anything, staring directly at Roger as if trying to read his thoughts.

'It would appear you have been spying on us? For whom? I am presuming on behalf of a Roundhead General. And please, don't disrespect me by lying,' she was polite and firm in her questioning. But Roger could sense an underlying ruthlessness in her tone.

'Yes, we have my lady,' Roger saw little point in denying the obvious. 'As from whom we take orders, I can't answer that.'
'Can't or won't?'

Roger remained silent, he looked away from her at the floor. Even through the veil, he could feel her eyes boring into him.

The woman changed her approach, 'You have a family?'

'Yes, my lady.'

She looked across the room to one of the guards, still hiding his face behind a kerchief. 'How long would it take to get to Risby and find this man's family?'

The guard paused for a moment, thinking. Then said, 'No more than two hours, my lady.'

Looking back at Roger she asked, 'So you have a choice, we can keep this discussion amongst ourselves or I can bring your family here, and I'm sure with some persuasion,' she motioned the guard towards the fire, where he picked up a glowing hot poker from the flames, putting it close to Roger's cheek, 'We can ask your wife the same question?'

The blood drained from Roger's face, sweat broke out on his forehead, his eyes filled with fear, 'My...my...lady, they know nothing, please do not harm them. They are innocent.'

'They may be, but you are not. By undertaking the actions you have, you put your family in danger as well. You have chosen the wrong side in this war. You and others will suffer accordingly. I have no hesitation in bringing them here if it helps loosen your tongue.'

'My lady please, please understand I know nothing of...' In his fear, Roger unthinkingly blurted out what his inquisitor wanted to hear. '... Major General Fleetwood's plans, our local commander Hezekiah Haynes gives us our orders. I know nothing more.'

'Ah! Now we have some names! Unfortunately for you, ones we already know. Who else have you been asked to spy on?'

Roger hesitated for a second before replying, 'No one else, my lady.'

'Your hesitation tells me you are paltering.' She turned to the guard, 'Go and fetch this lying wretch's family. Seeing them suffer may straighten his tongue into telling the truth.'

The prospect of seeing his wife and children tortured was too much, Roger resistance dissolved, 'No, no, please stop. I will tell you all I know. Please don't hurt my family!'

'A wise decision Roger of Risby. We are not the barbarians Cromwell would have you believe we are. We fight for our King to be back on the throne. Not to harm his people. Now tell me everything, and you and your friends will be free before the night's end.'

Roger told them all he knew, which wasn't a lot. He did reveal who else was on Hezekiah's watchlist and the names of some others like himself working as spies for the Roundheads. The lady interrogator seemed pleased with the information he provided, and true to her word, by sunrise Roger and his companions were thrown out of the house.

They quickly rode to Hezekiah's house in Stowmarket to tell him of their harrowing experience. Roger claimed they had escaped from the house, fabricating a story that made him and his fellow spies look brave and too clever for their captors. By the time Hezekiah and a dozen soldiers arrived back at the house, it was deserted. One of the soldiers suggested burning the royalist sanctuary to the ground. Wisely, Hezekiah ordered him to do no such thing. A house fire could easily take hold and reduce the area to ash and rubble. Instead, they ransacked it for anything of value, broke windows, doors and further ruined its once beautiful interior.

The Veiled Lady used the information extracted from Roger to warn the other Royalists to leave their homes for fear of their activities being spied upon, or worse being captured and tortured to reveal any fellow conspirators in the *Sealed Knot*.

The *Sealed Knot* continued its disorganised attempts at an insurrection to overthrow Cromwell's Protectorate. A rising later in 1655 was quashed by the Roundheads and the secret organisation became even more fragmented and ineffective. To combat the *Sealed Knot's* inability to launch a well orchestrated uprising, a splinter group called the *Action Party* came to the fore, promising to coordinate a successful revolt. It, too, failed to make an impact. Both the *Sealed Knot* and the *Action Party* were riven with disagreements and infiltrated by Cromwell's spies to be a serious threat to the Protectorate. In the end, Cromwell's death in 1658 and the failure of his son Richard to continue the Republic, led to Charles II being restored to the throne in 1660 and such secret organisations were disbanded.

The house, in its dilapidated condition, was left unoccupied until the new King came to the throne. Its secretive owner, taking advantage of the settled state of the country and an improving local economy, put the house up for sale.

The new buyers were familiar with the house, they had lived there years before`.

Chapter 23

~1660~

"My good Lord, what a mess, this poor house is nothing like the one we left over two decades ago. What a shame," lamented Joan as she stood outside, leaning on her walking stick, sadly looking up at its sagging roof, broken windows and faded paintwork.

'That's why we managed to buy it so cheaply,' explained her elder daughter Diane. 'We will make it as beautiful as it was in my grandmother's time. It is fortunate Benedict is a builder, so it should not take too long to make it habitable again.' Her voice was bubbling with excitement at the prospect of moving into the house she remembered visiting as a child. The vivid memories of drunken guests, laughter, the smell of beer and food, her grandmother, Maud and friend Grace keeping the Inn running smoothly and with such gaiety. They made a profound impression on her six-year-old mind, to see two such capable women in control of a successful business. She was determined to restore the house to its former glory—without the bar!

'Shall we go in and see what needs to be done?' suggested Diane.

They entered the great hall, now empty and forlorn. During its time as *The Gentlemen's Rest*, it featured a bar with booths and tables for the guests. Now all was stripped bare. The floorboards in many places were broken or rotted. The walls once a gleaming whitewash interspersed with the huge vertical oak beams, now were a dull, dirty brown. Instead of the convivial smells of the tavern, now it was malodorous, an overpowering aura of dampness, smoke, soot and...human waste. A culmination of neglect, years of no one living in and caring for the fabric, had taken away its soul. For a long time, it hadn't been a home, a place to be loved and cared for. Just a house, a building containing no love, no happiness. Diane shook off the feeling of malaise, determined to put right the wrongs and make it a proper, welcoming home once again.

They entered the south wing, or gable, once the kitchen area and servants' quarters. Now it was just three empty rooms, the one at the front facing the street still had a huge inglenook fireplace for cooking. All the beautiful cupboards containing a glittering array of copper utensils and pots had gone. Upstairs, the servant's rooms were equally devoid of any sign of care or maintenance. Damp patches on the floor and ceiling revealing tell tale signs of a leaking roof. Finally, the two attic rooms in the eaves of the house were full of cobwebs, rat droppings and bird nests—courtesy of a missing window.

'Oh heavens this is so depressing,' said Diane in a sad voice. It was worse, far worse than she expected.

'Don't worry my dearest,' consoled Benedict. 'It looks worse than it is, we can make this as good as new, I promise.' Diane wanted to believe her husband's optimistic promise, but she was beginning to have doubts about their purchase of the house. 'Cheer up, the north wing is in much better condition,' said Benedict, gently steering his wife down the stairs back to the great hall.

They walked past the magnificent fireplace, some ten feet across, still with its ornate stone mantle and a previous owner's coat of arms. The north wing was a mirror image of the south. With three downstairs rooms, in the past used as guest bedrooms, or, at one time, a study. Up the beautiful oak stairs, the balustrades carved with intricate floral designs, were the owner's quarters, bedroom, dressing room and on the top floor, storage rooms. As Benedict had said, these rooms showed less damage than in the south wing. The roof had held, not leaked, preventing any water damage. Diane breathed a silent sigh of relief.

The room above the great hall was empty except for the huge limestone chimney breast that kept it warm in winter when the fire below was lit. Frequently, past owners had slept here when it was too cold to use their own bedrooms.

Feeling more optimistic, they went back downstairs where Joan waited. Her arthritic knees preventing her from taking the grand tour. 'So, when do you hope to move in?" she asked.

Benedict thought for a moment, 'I think I can have this ready in about a month, with luck.'

240

Joan laughed, 'Ha, a builder's month is everyone else's six! I shall not start packing yet.'

Diane smiled, 'Probably a wise move mother. Sorry husband, I know your movable deadlines. As long as we are ready for the start of the school year, we can get both Oliver and Matthew enrolled, that is the most important thing. Also, I am sure my sister will be delighted to have the farm to themselves after all these years.'

Joan agreed, 'You're right, buying this house will allow them to develop the farm without us getting in the way. For me, to live in the town will make it easier to visit friends and grow old gracefully in some comfort. I am so grateful for you allowing me to stay with you. Farm living is for the young and fit. I am neither.'

Diane looked at Benedict, raising an eyebrow. They had little choice about the house sharing arrangements.   Joan had provided most of the money for the purchase, a condition of which was a room or two for her to live in. It was a fair trade they both agreed. It meant what little capital they'd saved could be used for renovating the house. But living with someone as demanding as Joan gave Diane some cause for concern. Hopefully the size of the house would mean they would not be bumping into one another all the time.

Tactfully Diane replied, 'We're delighted to have you here, mother. It's also another pair of hands to look after the house, and the boys!' With that comment she walked back out to the street leaving a slightly stunned Joan trailing behind. Grandmothers were not supposed to be unpaid housekeepers and nursemaids. Words would be had later, she told herself, as she hobbled after them.

*****

It was a double celebration—the builders were practically finished (after four months) repairing and decorating the house, just one of the bedrooms in the owner's wing needed more work. Plus, Plus, outside, a huge bonfire was being built to honour the new King Charles II's accession to the throne. After eleven years of Civil War and a failed attempt at running England as a Republic, the monarchy had been restored. The heavy handed puritanical rule of Cromwell did not sit well with many people, so even the excesses of past Kings were an acceptable alternative.

'Come let us put some of the old wood and rubbish from the building onto the bonfire,' ordered Diane to her two boys, Oliver aged seven, and Matthew, nine. Eagerly they gathered up some old wattle sticks and small broken floor boards, dragging them outside down the street to the bonfire—already over ten feet high and growing by the minute. It was an excellent way for everyone to get rid of unwanted items .

'It will be a huge fire mother. Will we be allowed to come outside and watch?'

'Of course Matthew, but only if I, or your father, are with you.' The boys agreed and ran back inside to grab some more wood for the fire.

Benedict was working hard upstairs, ripping out damp or damaged wall panelling when he noticed a section in good condition but with a thin cut separating it from the rest of the wall. Intrigued, he looked closer and saw a row of four panels could be removed in one piece. He picked up his turnscrew and gently levered the section. With some effort, it fell away from the rest of the wall, revealing a small storage area. At the back was a wooden box the size of a tea chest. Excited at his find, he reached in and dragged the box out. Its lid was held in place with hinges and a small clasp. It easily succumbed to a delicate hit with his hammer.

Benedict pulled up the top of the box and looked inside: there were dozens, no, probably hundreds of letters. He gently picked up one bundle, it was carefully tied together with a pink ribbon. Extracting one letter he opened it and started to read its contents. Then stopped, ran to the top of the stairs and shouted, 'Diane, come up here at once, I found something you'll want to see.'

An hour later, all three were sitting on the floor now surrounded by piles of letters taken from the box. 'They are the letters Grace wrote to my mother Maud. She couldn't speak, so this is how she communicated, though most read like a mixture of love letters and business reports. A strange combination," explained Joan, who had joined in the voyage of discovery Grace's letters had taken them.

Diane was reading one after another enraptured by the beautiful prose, the passion they conveyed and revealing in detail the amazing life these two women led. There had been talk that Maud and Grace were *tribads*, though a subject rarely discussed in polite society. Now here was the proof. But such

243

was the love they so clearly shared neither Diane, Joan, or even Benedict, passed any derogatory comments. They had been happy and discrete, who were the current generation to pass judgement?

'Oh my heavens mother, I think I have found one of the last *billet doux*, Grace wrote, it is so brief, yet so poignant, I believe I might start crying!' She read it, mainly for Benedict's sake as he was not competent with his reading.

'You have been my everything. I am blessed to have loved you. See you in heaven my angel. G.'

'Isn't that just so…touching, so…heartfelt…so sad?' said Diane, tears rolling down her cheeks.

'We all knew they loved each other dearly. These letters show the depth of their affection. I had no idea Grace kept this correspondence going for so many years, and that my mother saved them. They are truly a window into both their souls. Sadly, or perhaps not, my mother did indeed soon join her in heaven, she died only a few weeks after Grace, we all believed of a broken heart. I will read through these letters, I am such they will be fascinating. We must keep them safe, they are a precious find.'

'Well we'll leave you to your reminiscing mother, we have more rubbish for the bonfire to take out. Will you join us for the lighting later on?' asked Diane standing up and brushing the dust off her dress.

'Yes I will. Allow me a few minutes to read these letters, I am already discovering more about my mother than I ever knew. Anyway, it will be too dark to read soon.'

Later, soon after dark, the huge bonfire was lit. Some of the residents warned it was dangerous to have such a large fire so close to the houses. Disregarding their fears, more wood was thrown on and the flames leapt, snarling and curling twenty feet into the air.

People were in festive mood, a new King was a cause for celebration, especially after the uncertain, at times violent, oppressive rule of the Roundheads. The English were wedded to their monarch, even if at times like any marriage, its differences could flare up unpredictably and sometimes violently.

The beer was flowing, food was being cooked on the embers raked from the blaze, the residents of Whyting street were enjoying themselves. They were optimistic for the future.

Matthew and Oliver were running with other children round and round the bonfire, singing "Ring a ring a roses" even though it was not May Day when it was traditionally sung.

'You two be careful, don't get too close to the fire,' shouted Benedict to the boys. They waved at him and disappeared again behind the ever larger blaze.

Diane was becoming worried at the size of the bonfire and heat it was giving off. She stepped back to cool down, gently pulling Joan with her, 'Benedict, please get the boys here, I am fearful of the strength of this fire, it seems to be getting out of

245

control.' Even as she spoke, other revellers, oblivious to the potential danger, were still throwing more dried wood onto it, stoking the flames still further.

Benedict ran forward and caught both the boy's arms and hauled them back to his side. They were hot, out of breath, their cheeks rosy red. 'We were having fun father, why did you stop us?' complained Oliver, eyes shining with excitement, his long dark hair sticking with sweat to his forehead.

'We are worried the fire is getting too large, we don't want you too close until it has died down a little. Stay close to me, both of you,' Benedict ordered, shouting above the noise of the crowd and the crackling blaze.

Suddenly, a gust of wind funnelled by the narrow street gusted into the bonfire and like a giant bellow, caused the flames to intensify sending a cascade of sparks and embers flying into the air higher than the rooftops. Two unfortunate people caught by surprise close to the bonfire were now on the ground writhing in pain, their clothes alight. People rushed over to pull them away and smother the flames.

The atmosphere, quick as the blast of wind, turned from frivolity to fear. Everyone looked skywards to see where the embers were landing, if their roofs were in danger of catching alight. While none had thatch anymore, most of them were now covered in wooden shingles, baked dry by the summer sun.

'Benedict!' screamed Diane, 'Look!' She pointed to the roof of the north wing, some embers had lodged in the valley between the north gable and the central hall. Leaves caught there the previous autumn were brittle and dry. Like kindling, the smallest flame, fanned by the wind, would ignite them with ease. Ominously, small fires were already starting to burn. 'Benedict, do something! Hurry, our house will burn down!' Diane shouted in panic, gathering the children around her, she watched in helpless horror as the tiny flames grew in strength, inching up the valley to the ridge, gathering in strength as they did so.

Benedict was quick to see the danger. He ran inside and came out with his builder's ladder. He leant it against the eaves of the great hall and clambered up. The steep pitch of the roof made climbing up to where the fires were starting to take hold, slippery and dangerous. But he was too concerned about saving his house to worry for his safety. He reached the ridge of the roof and crawled towards the fires, now beginning to take hold. He reached the first fire, took off his shirt and quickly beat the flames out.

He slid down the valley between the roofs and repeated the process. Fifteen exhausting minutes later he put the last fire out. Cheers came from the crowd below as he completed the dangerous task. He smiled and waved at Diane and his children. Relief swept through them all, their precious new home was safe.

Benedict stayed up on the roof for the rest of the evening, until the bonfire in the street was just a pile of red hot embers and no longer a danger. Wearily, he climbed down the ladder, went inside and gulped down a pitcher of ale. He hugged his wife and children, thankful they still had a roof over their head, a home to live in.

The home that contained so many memories for his family was saved, yet again, from ruination.

Chapter 24 -

~The Future~

For the next two hundred years, the house in Whyting street would be home to people living through equally turbulent times. A snapshot, a microcosm, of England as it progressed from the Middle Ages to Victorian times.

The future would see its succession of owners and residents face their own trials, tribulations, successes and failures against the backdrop of the Industrial Revolution, England's rise as a global power, continuing unrest within the Monarchy, and the transition to the stable Victorian era.

One thing that wouldn't change, until one momentous day in 1735, were the tragic effects of Spinster Wordsworth's 250 year old spell on the house. Finally, the tragedies that befell so many children would be banished to the past. The house was at last freed from its evil burden, allowing future generations to live unencumbered by a witch's revenge.

And the enigmatic lettering young Harold found carved on a stone deep in the tunnels under the town?. They would lead to a discovery that shook Bury to its very foundations.

But that's another story.

The End

ABOUT THE AUTHOR

Paul Rowney was born 1954, in London, England and moved to America in 2004. I am now a US Citizen. Married with two children and five step children and 11 grandchildren.

At home I have seven dogs and various other two and four legged friends to keep me company on the small farm we live on near Nashville, Tennessee.

I have previously published three 'post apocalyptic' books:

French Creek.

A Return to the 21st Century, and

S.O.S .The Storm of all Storms.

(all are available on <u>Amazon</u> or via my website: <u>www.paulhrowney.com</u>)

The fourth book in the *French Creek* series will come out in 2024.

The sequel to *The Crown Post* will be published in late 2024.

Dear Reader,

Firstly, thank you for buying, and reading this book. Could I ask a huge favour of you?

If you have enjoyed The Crown Post, please take just a minute or two to write a review on my Amazon page. Your comments help others decide whether to purchase the book and also provides me with valuable feedback.

If you have any questions or comments, please do write to me via my website: www.paulhrowney.com

Thank you, Paul H Rowney.

Printed in Great Britain
by Amazon

36211842R00139